A

Originally from Woodstock, New York, Raphaela Weissman studied French and creative writing at New York University and in Paris. *Monsters* is her first novel, and her fiction and nonfiction work has been published in *L* Magazine, *New York Press*, *Bookslut*, *Gallatin Review*, GeekWire, *Publishers Weekly* and the *Euphony Journal*. She has worked as a literacy teacher, a campaign fundraiser, a community organizer, a tech sector drone, an amateur comedian, a bankruptcy specialist, a salesperson, and a video transcriber for various reality TV programming. She lives in Seattle, Washington, with her three beautiful plants.

MONSTERS

Raphaela Weissman

MONSTERS

RAPHAELA WEISSMAN

This edition first published in 2018

Unbound

6th Floor Mutual House, 70 Conduit Street, London W1S 2GF

www.unbound.com

ISBN (eBook): 978-1-911586-75-3

ISBN (Paperback): 978-1-911586-74-6

Design by Mecob

Cover image:
© Shutterstock

To Lisa, Melani, and Joe

Dear Reader,

The book you are holding came about in a rather different way to most others. It was funded directly by readers through a new website: Unbound.

Unbound is the creation of three writers. We started the company because we believed there had to be a better deal for both writers and readers. On the Unbound website, authors share the ideas for the books they want to write directly with readers. If enough of you support the book by pledging for it in advance, we produce a beautifully bound special subscribers' edition and distribute a regular edition and e-book wherever books are sold, in shops and online.

This new way of publishing is actually a very old idea (Samuel Johnson funded his dictionary this way). We're just using the internet to build each writer a network of patrons. Here, at the back of this book, you'll find the names of all the people who made it happen.

Publishing in this way means readers are no longer just passive consumers of the books they buy, and authors are free to write the books they really want. They get a much fairer return too – half the profits their books generate, rather than a tiny percentage of the cover price.

If you're not yet a subscriber, we hope that you'll want to join our publishing revolution and have your name listed in one of our books in the future. To get you started, here is a £5 discount on your first pledge. Just visit unbound.com, make your pledge and type THOMAS18 in the promo code box when you check out.

Thank you for your support,

Dan, Justin and John
Founders, Unbound

Super Patrons

Silke Anderson
Rachael Bacha
Melani Baker
Lisa Baker
Michael & Geri Baker
Cafe Barjot
Becks Bee
Rachel Bloom
Dave Blundell
Stuart & Nancy Braman
Lisa Brooks
Emily Campbell
Helen Chandler
Jordan Compton
Margaret Decker
Magan Do
William Doane
Caitlin Donovan
Maurice Downes
Robbin Ezinga
Adam Feinberg
Anna Wurtz & Matt Fried
Katie Garrison
Adam Greenwood
Juliana de Groot
John Haney
Jan Hansen
Melissa Hjorten
Pamela Holzer
Leonard Jones
David Jones
Dave Juchau

Janiece Jungell
Stephanie Kallos
Ide Katims
Mary Katz
Clive Kewell
Dan Kieran
Gillie Kindel
Danelle Knapp
Dietrich Knauth
Kara Lander
Joe Leonard
Penelope Levine
Benjamin Lim
Lisa Locascio
James Longbotham
Tim Manley
Helena Marchetti
Roy Marin
Aaron Martin
Mary McClellan
Jessica McKay
Alison McKay
Elizabeth Sulzbach & Drew Mickus
John Mitchinson
AJ Morales
Peter Mountford
Abram Mueller
Alex Muro
Roland Nenno
Eric Neubauer
Erik Nevala-Lee
Ashley Palar
Fran Pargament
Lou Perez
Justin Pollard
Danial Rushton

Theresa Safe
Carolyn Sas
Amy Savage
Ryan Scatenato
Hannah Sherrard
Rita Sherry
Holly Smith
Anna Staab
Laurel Staab
Linda Still
Tabatha Stirling
Daniel Strong
Annika Umbinetti
Patricia Ward
Ben Weber
Nicole Weissman
Peter Weissman
Andrew Weissman
Benjamin Wellington
Valerie Whitaker

With grateful thanks to Rita Sherry, who helped make this book happen.

Sometimes, the man would still get the desire to travel, but he could not bring himself to start out. What was the point of going on a trip that led nowhere?

—Yiddish folk tale

PART I

Brooklyn, Fall 2002

1

The first time it happened was in the spring. She'd woken up at the staircase, gripping the railing and staring down. Paul only stirred when she climbed back into bed. She was cold and sweaty; her hands still felt the phantom curve of wood against her palms, pressing into her skin with an urgency she didn't understand. "Mm?" he'd breathed, turning towards her.

Then she made a mistake.

She could have said nothing; why did she even decide that his noise was a question? He could have just been half-awake and happy to feel her there. But she was half-awake too, in a way she'd never felt before, one foot still deeply implanted in her dream life, the rest of her more aware of the tangible world around her than she'd ever been this late at night. But, for whatever reason, it seemed imperative to interact with the living thing next to her, so, question or not, she'd answered, almost immediately.

"I think I just sleepwalked." The silence beside her came alive; there was no doubt that Paul was wide awake. "I woke up at the railing."

Their room was quiet enough that any movement echoed in the bed language of sheets and springs, but even though she heard nothing, she knew he'd moved away. The pressure of his arm, that tingly warmth that happens when two sets of skin barely share a surface, was gone, just gone; he didn't even leave a phantom, like the banister.

It had happened four times since then, that she knew about. Once she was in the bathroom, once halfway down the stairs. Once she woke up staring at herself in the mirror above the dresser in their room, which was so terrifying she'd stopped breathing as soon as she woke up; and, most recently, she'd awoken in the middle of the living room, Paul holding her arm from what seemed like a great distance.

And there was the time in France. But she didn't like to think about that one, so she didn't count it.

But there could have been other times, too. How would she know? She'd had to accept that she didn't truly know herself the way she thought she did; some part of her went for walks in the middle of the night, responded to a voice other than her own. She couldn't presume things about this other person, the sleeping version of her. Maybe she went for a stroll every single night, and the times she knew about were only moments when she'd behaved badly. Maybe her normal routine bordered on harmlessness, a dream walk around the room before returning to the bed silently, without so much as rumpling the sheets.

Paul didn't know. For all his hyped-up concern, he never kept a vigil. He slept soundly through the night, which Annie thought was his way of rubbing it in.

As long as Thomas couldn't hear or see his parents, he couldn't be sure they were there. He stood in the hallway outside the living room, where they may or may not have been sitting, waiting for him.

When he wasn't looking, his parents—all adults, maybe—turned into monsters. It was completely possible. There are things you learn between the ages of eight (like him) and forty (like them). One of them could be how to change into something else. There could be some button in his body that wouldn't grow in until he was twenty-seven—you press it, and you're a monster, when your kid's out of the room.

All his life, his parents could have been turning into monsters, every time he blinked. As they served him dinner or tucked him in at night, they could be thinking about eating him.

Thomas didn't totally understand how it worked yet. He thought you probably had to go to some secret place to become a monster, that adults went there for just a split second before they changed, disappeared and came back. He thought that place probably felt like a dream, except that when your brain takes you there, you're really there, and you can actually do stuff. He'd be able to steer the plane, for example, if he wanted to. He could stop it from crashing.

That disappearing time was the scariest part about people becoming monsters. Thomas thought it might be possible to get stuck there.

When his parents were monsters, even very hungry monsters, at least they were still there; he might still be able to reach them. If he caught them as monsters, he'd just look them in the eyes and say, "Hey, it's me. Can't you see that? It's just me." They couldn't argue with something as simple and true as that. They'd have to change back.

But if they disappeared, there was nothing he could do. He wouldn't know where to look. If he wanted to, he could open the front door and wander out into Brooklyn, right now. Nothing was stopping him. He could do it any night. Any of them could. The fact that it was dangerous out there wasn't enough to bolt the door from the inside. It was like what had happened last year, when the airplanes crashed into the buildings—everyone kept saying they couldn't believe it, they couldn't believe it, but that wasn't enough to stop it from happening. If his parents disappeared, for good, it would be so scary that Thomas couldn't imagine it, but it could happen, all right. For all he knew, it could happen that night.

2

Annie wasn't sure how she'd come to be married to a man who felt proprietary about a chair. Yet there he was, outlined in faded violet, looking so pleased with himself it was like no one had ever sat in a comfortable seat before. Her place was on the opposite couch, observing the domestic calm over which he reigned, while Thomas played with his trucks at his father's feet. This was what it was all about now.

In the evenings, she wished for a leaky faucet or a distant screaming baby to provide some sound. The quiet made her uneasy. When she was in her twenties, living not so far from here, in bordering Brooklyn neighborhoods rougher around the edges, she and her roommates would compete to be heard over the sound of trucks backfiring on the BQE, or the B61 bus, which was never around when she needed it but somehow always managed to roar up and down their block at two o'clock in the morning. Having a steady salary afforded them the luxury of a shadier street, a full brownstone to themselves, and a disquieting insulation from the very same noises, only a few blocks away.

Paul and Thomas could remain silent for hours, so any major shift in the living room's molecules fell to her. She'd appreciated that about Paul when they first met: there was something so smart about a thin, plain-faced guy listening to everyone else speak, waiting for the appropriate moment to say something worthwhile. Recently, she'd grown to resent all of it, a piece at a time: his thinness had translated to smugness, somehow, like there was less of him on purpose, so that he could be less affected by the things around him. His quiet was also problematic, now that it was rubbing off on their son. Before she was a mother, Annie had found quiet children creepy, and had imagined her own child would be a nonstop geyser of noise and life and snot and chaos.

Her restlessness called up such pangs of being eight or nine years old, trapped in temple on the high holy days, that her clothes seemed to shrink and stiffen around her. And just as she'd done when she was little and awoke in the middle of the night after a bad dream, she remained still, imagining what her small voice would sound like in the darkness as it broke the evening air.

"Paul," she said finally. The sound of her voice wasn't welcome, like something hard to see had been dropped from the ceiling.

Paul didn't answer.

Now that the seal had been broken, speaking came easier. "*Paul.*"

From behind the front page of the newspaper came a barely audible syllable. "Hmm?"

The arrogance of it—*Hmm.* His smug little utterances fit in well with the stifling quiet.

"I found another cockroach today," she said. "In the kitchen."

At this Thomas's head lifted and turned towards her, waiting. She smiled at him, grateful to see his face; Paul remained, for all intents and purposes, a talking newspaper.

"Mmm," Paul said, still hidden. "That's not good."

For an awful moment, silence settled back in, and she felt like a dog retrieving a stick for someone who didn't want to play. To her relief, he continued, and put the newspaper down. "Well, we tried the traps," he said. "I guess it's time to call an exterminator."

She used to see him as a beautifully simple creature. He'd been made of reason and quiet jokes and a gentle love that didn't call attention to itself but never went anywhere, and his face had seemed frozen in childhood, with wide open eyes and uncomplicated features still waiting to be filled in by age. He looked bored now, his eyes dull, not looking at anything.

Thomas turned towards his father, then back to her. "What's an exterminator?"

"He's a man who kills insects," Paul answered for her. His face softened, his eyes focusing, as he spoke to their son. "Pests. Little creepy crawlies that are in your house but shouldn't be there."

Thomas frowned down at his trucks, like he didn't find this answer entirely satisfactory. Annie was always struck by how transparently his face displayed his thoughts. People called him precocious, and told her and Paul that he seemed older than he was, but Annie thought the compliment was glib, and inaccurate. Her son wasn't an old-seeming kid, but, really, two people in one. He was a child and an adult, and if there was anything precocious about him it was his ability to maneuver between the two so fluidly. When he turned back to Annie, his face was eight years old again. He was grinning with his mouth open; the one missing tooth in his top row made all the rest look uneven, and gave him a look of sweetly sloppy innocence. "Can I see the cockroach?" he asked.

"It's not there anymore, kiddo," Paul said, retreating behind the newspaper.

"We don't know that," Annie said. She walked over to Thomas and made a clumsy grab at his hand. "In fact, let's go look now and see if it's there."

Paul put the paper back down to glare at her. He started to speak, but didn't. She could tell he was contemplating getting up, and that he was conflicted; the philosophy of the chair was that it was a place you settled into at the beginning of the evening and dialed your body down until it was time for bed.

"Let's go," she said, tugging at Thomas's hand. "Come on, let's go."

They looked for a long time. His mom could be nice that way, letting him do the weird things he wanted to do. Sometimes his parents didn't like how weird he was. Parents weren't supposed to care about stuff like that, were they?

Once Thomas had asked his best friend Ingrid if her parents minded that she was weird. She'd looked kind of upset. "I'm not weird."

"Not like bad weird. Not like when kids at school call us weird to be mean. But we're weird. You know."

They were in her room, eating rice cakes with peanut butter on a Snoopy towel on the floor. "Are you mad at me?" he asked.

"No. But I don't think I want to be weird."

"I don't know if I want to be either, but I don't think—" She really did look mad. "Never mind," he said. Ingrid picked up a rice cake and examined it; Thomas knew she was trying to see if there was enough peanut butter covering it to bother eating it. Plain rice cakes tasted terrible.

"I thought you didn't like Snoopy," he said after a minute.

"I don't," she'd said, frowning at his face on the towel. "He doesn't talk, and he's too silly."

In the kitchen, Thomas's mom said, "Hold on, I have an idea." She went to the cabinet where they kept random stuff, like cleaning supplies and extra bottled water.

"Here," she said. She handed him a flashlight. It was heavy and yellow and had his name on it. His mom had let him write it there because he liked the way it looked, even though it wasn't really his. "Shine it under the refrigerator. I bet he's hiding there. Be quick, though. They don't like light, so he'll probably try to run away."

Thomas got down on his hands and knees. He looked back up at his mom, backwards. She nodded. "Good," she said. "That's it."

He didn't turn the flashlight on right away. It was so dark he couldn't even see dust, but he knew it was there because he could smell it. Darkness was scary, but turning the light on was scarier. When he did, the cockroach, whatever it was, would be right up close. Then, his mom had said, it would run away and disappear; just like the monsters.

Thomas wondered if his mom was a monster right now, standing behind him. Maybe that was why she'd brought him in here in the first place; maybe she wanted to eat him, and she didn't want to share with his dad.

He turned around again. She was still his mom.

"You OK?" she said.

Thomas nodded.

"We don't have to do this, if you don't want to."

Thomas shook his head. "I want to."

He really did want to see it; he was scared, but that kind of made him want to see it more. He wanted to catch a real live monster in the act. His parents were way too fast for him. He pushed his thumb into the big rubber button on the flashlight, and it clicked as he let go.

He saw it right away. It turned and looked at him. Thomas knew it wasn't really looking, that it probably didn't have eyes the way humans did—his dad had taught him that—but it felt that way. It was bigger than he had imagined, maybe even the size of his thumb. He should have asked his dad if cockroaches bit, like mosquitoes; it looked like the kind of thing that could bite. Its antennae wiggled up and down, like they were reaching for him.

It's so close, Thomas thought, and then he realized that it was always close, even when he wasn't looking under the refrigerator. They lived in the same house, he and the cockroach. Whenever it wanted to, it could decide to leave the kitchen and come up the stairs...

"See anything?" his mom asked.

Her voice surprised him. He'd kind of forgotten she was there. He turned back to her, and when he looked back under the fridge, the cockroach was gone. He could hear its feet scraping against the floor, fast, like little drum beats.

"It was cool," Thomas said. He heard his father saying something in the other room. He kept the flashlight on, wondering if it might come back.

3

Paul watched his wife and son walk away from him and into the kitchen. Their gaits matched each other: Annie set a giddy pace, and Thomas, trotting along like a normal kid, looked like a little animal mimicking the bigger version, for no other reason than because she was the thing that nourished him.

He'd met her twelve years ago, when he'd begun teaching chemistry at Brooklyn College, where she was getting her Masters in English. His image of her at twenty-seven, when he'd met her, was a blurry agglomeration of bright skirts and scarves, thick curly brown hair which fell out of whatever kerchief she'd fashioned for herself in uneven chunks, and her round face shining out from behind all that earthy artifice with smart, smirking resolve. That was the funny thing about her in those early years, the endearing quality that, ultimately, made him fall in love: she worked so hard building up the accessories which she thought formed the bedrock of her bohemian appeal, but, secretly, Paul never cared for any of it, hardly even noticed. He wondered if she'd ever figured that out.

She'd gone through different phases, though she never strayed too far from left-of-center and whatever was in fashion for self-proclaimed freethinkers; in other words, she never dressed like him. Paul always suspected that part of her interest in him was just another quirky artifact, that the idea of dating someone square and preppy was cute, or funny. That's why it was hard for him to pin down answers to questions like why he loved her and what had stayed the same through all those years, because with Annie there was always a layer of intent, a consciousness of how things would look to some invisible audience; the difference between what she was really passionate about and what just seemed like a neat idea.

Now, for example: he knew that if she were thinking clearly, she wouldn't be dragging their son off to look at an enormous bug which would, more likely than not, exacerbate his already frequent nightmares. On matters of parenting, whenever he thought they were finally on the same page about something, she'd get impulsive—a magic word which had defined her for him in the beginning—and let it all go in favor of an ill-advised move like this. A field trip to the kitchen to see a little monster. As if their son didn't have enough unexplained images crawling around in his head already—people jumping out of windows to spare themselves from fiery deaths a few subway stops away from where he lived, and now a prehistoric bug in the house where he slept.

They came back into the living room, holding hands. "I saw it," Thomas said. "It was so big."

More and more, recently, he felt that his role was to wait patiently as Annie got something like this out of her system, then step in as the real parent. "Not as big as us," Paul said. "And now he knows we've got our eye on him."

"So now we call the—what's he called?"

He imagined Thomas peering through the kitchen doorway, watching as a strange man in a mask sprayed their house with poison. "Mom said I could watch," he'd say.

"I'll go buy some roach traps tomorrow," Paul said. "Those work pretty well."

He pulled his son gently away from Annie's hand and scooped him up in his arms. "All right, Bug Man," he said, "I think it's your bedtime." Thomas nodded and scrambled down to hug his mother.

"I'll be up in a minute," Paul called after Thomas as he ran out of the room and up the stairs. The noise of his footfalls grew muted, and he and Annie were alone. Some other time, this might have been a moment of relief for him and his wife, or one of love, or even sexual excitement; now, losing Thomas from the room felt like losing a net.

"What was that?" he asked, louder than he had intended.

When she spoke, her voice was dull and sleepy, and she didn't look at him. "I don't know." To his annoyance, she smirked. "What was what?"

"He's going to have nightmares," Paul said. She didn't look at him; his words hit her neck. "He just got over the nightmare thing."

"I don't like talking about him like this." She was loud now, too. "When he's not here."

"I don't want to have this argument again," Paul said. "He's eight years old. We're his parents. We don't owe him an audience with us when we want to discuss something we're concerned about."

She sighed, put-upon, like a teenager. "Fine, Paul."

"Please, just, don't scare our son, all right? He doesn't need scaring. That much I know."

He also knew it was a father's job to tell his scared son that there was nothing to be afraid of, and he'd had trouble with that part lately. He didn't say that to her.

"Look," he said, "are you... feeling all right?"

The way she looked at him sideways, as if he was a stranger pretending to be someone who knew her, told him that she knew exactly what he meant. "I'm feeling fine," she said. Sometimes her hazel eyes glowed, and sometimes, like now, they turned soupy and almost weren't there.

"You know what I mean," he said. "Have you been feeling OK recently?"

A half smile formed as she looked at him. It crept up the side of her face incrementally. "You tell me," she said. "Right?"

His son's small, clean voice came from upstairs, saving him. "Dad, I'm ready!"

The relief must have showed, because before he could say anything, she said, "Go." He attempted a smile and squeezed her shoulder. For a moment, things felt normal; it felt good to remember that their son was upstairs, that he was what mattered.

Then, once his back was turned, she added, "Don't worry. I'll tie myself to the bed."

Annie was the first girl he'd dated for longer than a few months. When he was in his twenties, he'd lie in bed next to various short-lived girlfriends and wonder what it would be like to get to the point where someone knew him so well she could read his face and draw from a store of knowledge about what he needed to hear depending on how he moved and breathed that day. He realized now that he'd overlooked the other part of it: she'd know exactly where to go to destroy him, the most efficient way to get there and exactly how much damage she could do. When Annie wanted to assure him that the things he spent every waking moment worrying about were the worries of a small, foolish man, she could do it effortlessly.

He stopped, trying to think of what to say. She was smiling at him, glancing down at her nails, as if this was some perverse flirtation.

"I'll see you upstairs," he said, and knew he had to move then or he wouldn't at all.

After he tucked Thomas in, he paused outside their bedroom, listening at the door. He felt evil; this was not how a husband was supposed to approach his wife. But ever since the sleepwalking started, he'd become aware of how much happened when he wasn't watching, and he'd become sneakier in general, trying to catch things by staying out of sight in his own house. What if the key to this whole sleepwalking problem was some activity so simple she wasn't even aware she did it—humming, grinding her teeth, brushing her hair a certain way? On hospital dramas, doctors sent crews to the patient's house to go over every inch of their life to see what they'd overlooked in the oblivion of routine. It was his duty to be aware of the things she couldn't.

He heard nothing but breathing, and the gliding of sheets. The gliding of sheets...

He cleared his throat. "You're not making the bed, are you?"

A floorboard creaked with a finality that suggested she'd just stood up straight and stopped moving. He imagined her staring straight ahead, responding to the sound of his voice like a startled animal.

"Yeah," she said from the other side of the wall. Her voice tilted in the direction of a question. "I thought... I don't know, I like everything to be as restful as possible. I guess I thought it would help." She seemed to be waiting for him to respond, but he couldn't think of anything to say, and still couldn't bring himself to enter the room.

He was startled when she spoke again. "Do you not want the bed made, Paul?"

"Don't—" he began, and knew it was time to face her. "Don't do that." When he entered the room, she looked as he'd imagined, holding the corner of what seemed like a grotesquely massive sheet limply in one hand, letting most of it drag on the floor. Only the bedside lamp was on, and she was backlit by dim light that made it seem too late for two people to still be awake, having a conversation. "You know I don't care," he said, not moving from the doorway. "I care about you getting better. I just think it's funny, making the bed when we're about to sleep in it and mess it up again."

"I don't know what I'm supposed to do, Paul. I don't know anything about it. I only know what happens to me." Her voice was small and soft from the other side of the room. At the moment, she looked perfect, in a way. She'd changed into her white nightgown, something she'd had since college but had recently unearthed, maybe because it went so well with the image of a woman wandering dark halls at night. In the bare lamplight, she was gray and luminescent, like a ghost who'd found her way to an unsuspecting family and was trying to leave. Her beauty, now, was classic and delicate, which was never how he'd thought of her. Now there was another person lying next to him at night; he only wished that this new person would give him a new opportunity at love, the way it had been before, light and effortless, but she was surrounded by something impenetrably sad and serious; he couldn't even touch her.

His mouth felt dry. The silence between them almost buzzed. "What *keeps* happening to you," he said, almost in a whisper.

She looked at him for a moment, and when she spoke, she was even quieter. "Right."

"First on the stairs, then in the bathroom, probably three or four times when I didn't wake up—" He knew it was cruel to go through the litany again. They both had it memorized.

"That's enough," she said, with a firmness he thought she'd abandoned downstairs. "Look, I told you I was willing to sleep in the living room, if this bothers you so much."

"Are you kidding?" The words Paul felt welling up inside him were things he'd promised himself he wouldn't say to her, the kind of gory paranoid fantasies he'd been thinking about since this all started. "I don't want you wandering out the door and into the night. Some neighbor finds you under a bridge tomorrow morning, or worse, nobody—"

"Please don't talk about me like I'm a dog you have to take care of."

He felt everything he hated to feel when he went to bed: unclean and angry and disgusted. He wondered if he'd get up and start wandering around too, out of sheer dissatisfaction. "OK," he said, as gently as he could. "I'll help you make the bed."

They made their bed in silence. It was the most lovely, pure married act they'd shared in a long time. He wished he could impose a permanent silence over their house; it always made things better. When they'd finished, she crawled into her side of the bed and he changed into his pajamas with his back to her, then slid between the sheets, faced away from her, and turned off the lamp on his nightstand, leaving them in darkness. Neither of them said "Good night" or touched each other; it took all the restraint he had not to lay his arm across her, to anchor her down, to make sure she was still there.

4

Thomas's stomach stayed in a tight ball until the muffled pillowy noises of his parents stopped. Then the ball moved up into his chest. It was nighttime, and he was alone.

He closed his eyes, because he knew that was what he was supposed to do, but he didn't want to. He squeezed them shut, squeezed his whole face tight, so nothing from the outside could get in. His room was cold; under the covers, his body could hide, but his face didn't want to be under there, and the cold air knew it and smothered his skin like an invisible blanket. *Please not the airplane dream*, he thought, *not the airplane dream, not the airplane dream.*

Thomas hoped his brain wouldn't get confused and think he was asking for the airplane dream, instead of wishing it away. At night, his dad had explained to him, the brain gets confused and does what it wants. It doesn't listen the way the daytime brain does. It made perfect sense to Thomas. How could the brain he trusted to help him with homework and remembering important stuff turn around and decide to do something like the airplane dream?

In the dream, it was the airplane from when they'd gone to France that summer, the only airplane he'd ever been on. Everything was blue and green and plastic or fabric, and there was a lot of space but everyone was crowded together. Everything was still but they were all moving. They were sitting in a big tin box where something could just pick them up out of the air and start shaking them, if it wanted to. He didn't know anyone, except his parents, and everyone was a grown-up or a baby. Just old faces and baby faces, which aren't even really faces yet, more like little pink cakes, scrunching down then opening up again. All the babies were crying or sleeping, and all the adults were sleeping or staring straight ahead. It was like nobody cared about anything, even though they were spinning through the air faster than a car could ever go (his dad had told him that).

There was no noise on the plane, only the roar of the engine. One huge loud noise that made everything seem silent. How did it do that? When Thomas was on the plane to France he'd wondered about that, why everyone made such a big deal about the fact that a plane could fly and no one even seemed to notice the noise thing, that it stopped all the other sounds while being the loudest machine Thomas had ever heard. That was amazing. But no one cared.

In the dream, Thomas knew that the plane was going to crash, but he was the only one who knew. He knew it suddenly, like he'd just remembered that he'd left his lunch at home. A little idea occurred to him: *the plane's going to crash.* And he knew it was true. He didn't know how he was so sure of that, but in the dream it was clear, there was just no doubt at all, that plane was definitely going to crash.

He was sitting between his mother and his father, and they were acting like all the other adults on the plane: his mother was staring straight ahead, and his father was sleeping. He didn't know how to get their attention to tell them, but he knew he had to. He tried his mother first, since she was at least awake. He tapped her hand over and over again, but she just kept staring straight ahead, so when that didn't work he started slapping the back of her hand, hard, harder than he wanted to. She wouldn't look down. He grabbed his father's arm and shook it, telling him to wake up, but his father wouldn't wake up. He grabbed each of their arms and shook as hard as he could. He started yelling, "The plane's gonna crash! Help!" and his voice was the loudest thing on the plane, louder than the engine even, but his parents still couldn't hear him, and the other people on the plane started to disappear. Thomas could hardly see them anymore; only the backs of their heads. It was like they weren't there.

Then, finally, he began to feel it, the big dipping down. The motor noise changed; it started to grind around and get louder and quieter. It sounded like the entire plane was going to puke. All the green and blue and plastic was sliding around and becoming a big gray soup, and no one was there except him and his parents.

And they finally looked down at him, both of them, and his mother said, "The plane is crashing," and they both just sat there, staring at him. Nobody moved.

Then he'd wake up.

He'd had bad dreams before, but none he hated like this one. He wished his dad hadn't told him that dreams were just a part of his own brain, because now he knew he was just stuck with the airplane dream for as long as his stupid brain wanted to keep it there.

In the middle of the night, in the middle of her sleep, Annie heard the unmistakable tinkly strains of the Mister Softee song. She often told Thomas, with considerable pride, that this particular song hadn't changed since she was his age, and that if there was anything she knew for certain in this world, it was that it never would change. In less civilized parts of the world—like New Hampshire, where Paul was from—ice cream men settled for "Pop Goes the Weasel" or "Turkey in the Straw." Only New York had its own ice cream song, the undying anthem of summer.

Somewhere in her half-consciousness, a memory surfaced: there was a kid in her third-grade class whose father drove a Mister Softee truck, and had taught him the secret words to the song. She felt her mouth moving to form the words:

The creamiest, dreamiest soft ice cream
You get from Mister Softee.
For a refreshing delight supreme,
Look for Mister Softee.

The song continued—if the Mister Softee song ever stopped, it wouldn't be the Mister Softee song—and Annie felt herself breathing quickly, certain that she would wake up any minute.

This happened sometimes, recently, as she became fluent in the new nighttime language of her body and her mind. Towards the end of a dream, or what felt more like a vision—a frozen picture of her house, the apartment of her childhood, the bookstore where she worked, precise scenes in every detail except that she was always alone—she'd get the sense that she had walked. It wasn't anything tangible, like cold air or the feel of her feet on the floor. It was the memory of a feeling, like phantom pains from an old injury. It wasn't good or bad. She didn't do anything when she felt it; just accepted the information from herself, like someone was answering a question she'd asked a long time ago and then forgotten.

She awoke to a shock of damp cold, originating from her head and running through her limbs. She was standing at their bedroom window, her arms splayed out on either side, bracing herself against the windowsill, her forehead pressed against the glass. Annie blinked her eyes into focus. She was staring at the traffic of President Street, which, at this hour—4:30am? 5am?—was nonexistent, except for the Mister Softee truck making its way west, towards the BQE.

Could you even buy an ice cream cone at this hour, if you wanted to? she wondered as she snuck back into bed, where Paul was snoring lightly, oblivious to her absence. *Go figure.*

When Thomas woke up, he thought he was going to throw up. His whole body shot up out of the dream, as if something was trying to push itself out of him. Something wasn't right.

He didn't remember the dream at all. It might have been the airplane dream, or something completely new. It was dark and quiet, and something wasn't right.

He heard the ice cream truck outside. That song was playing. Thomas wished that meant it was daytime—who would eat ice cream in the middle of the night?—but there was no sunlight peeking in through his curtains, only the dirty orange of the streetlamp.

There was some creaking and rustling coming from his parents' room next door. Thomas liked that. Monsters or not, someone was there. He lay back down and closed his eyes, happy to know that at least that much was true.

5

Thomas did his homework on the living room floor. They'd spent too much money on the desk which lived upstairs in his room and which he never used, but Annie didn't mind. She liked it when he did his homework like this, his school stuff sprawled out on the beige carpet in front of him, lying on his stomach and kicking his legs in the air. He looked like a little boy, not a miniature man, which is how he looked at that desk. Sometimes, like tonight, she'd position herself on the couch with a magazine and pretend to read. She'd watch his little hands moving, the golden-brown hair on his little head, and imagine what thoughts were in there.

"Thomas," she said, "stop for a second." He made an adorable maneuver to face her—dropped his legs down then twisted himself around so that he was lying on his back and sat up from there. It was ungraceful and unnecessary. She wanted to pick him up and cradle him to her. "Is something bothering you?" she asked.

"No," he said. His right eyebrow drooped, like he didn't quite buy what she was saying. The man in boy's clothing had returned.

"I don't mean right now," she said. "I just mean in general, in your life. Are you doing OK?"

"Yes," said Thomas. His face didn't move.

Annie lowered herself off the couch, so that she was sitting against it, on the floor, at his level. The carpet was surprisingly soft; she wondered how she'd lived there for nine years and never had occasion to sit on the living room floor. "Because... well, do you think you would tell me if something was wrong?"

Now his face changed. His adult's dubiousness became a child's confusion. She loved watching those tiny shifts in the right direction, when his whole face opened up and let innocence flood back in from wherever it had been hiding. "What do you mean?" he asked.

She tried to think of the simplest way to explain what she meant. "You're eight now."

"Yeah. I'll be nine in April."

"Right," she said. "That's a long time, eight years. That's how long I've known you. And I can't remember anything ever bothering you. At least, you've never told me that something's been bothering you. Don't you think that's strange?"

His eyes shifted away from her, like he was looking for some distraction to save him. She didn't mind; little kids were supposed to be restless. "I don't know," he said after a minute.

She could see that he didn't understand. This was what happened with Thomas; she'd enter into a conversation with the adult, only to be answered by the little boy. She started over again.

"Thomas," she asked, gently, like someone who was trying to be a good mother, "have you been having nightmares again?"

She thought she saw something shift in his eyes, but it happened fast. Maybe this was what growing up was going to be like for him: less and less perceptible movements between the child and the adult, until one day, she wouldn't be able to tell the difference. "No," he said, then looked away from her before adding, "not for a while."

"OK. But, you know, if you are, you can tell me. I think talking about it might help." She couldn't tell from his expression whether or not he understood. "Talking to me," she added. "You know, I have nightmares too, sometimes."

"You do?"

"Sure. Unfortunately, they don't always go away when you get older. Especially if something really scary happens—like what happened last year, with the airplanes. I had nightmares about that for a while. Did you?"

She imagined if Paul knew about this conversation, he would find fault with it. She found herself leaning in and whispering, like they were sharing gossip.

Thomas hesitated for a moment, looking at her as if he were trying to make up his mind about something. Finally, he gave a tiny nod.

She wanted to ask for more details, but it had been hard enough getting this much out of him. "OK," she said. "See? Scary things give everyone bad dreams. So I just thought—" She turned towards the staircase. Paul had announced earlier that he was going to his study, so given his adolescent demands for solitude when he was there, as if he were some misunderstood genius composing a great work of art, she knew he likely wouldn't appear in their midst anytime soon. "I'm sorry I showed you that cockroach, Thomas," she said. "That was probably scary, and if it gave you a nightmare, that's my fault."

"It didn't," he said. He was getting a little squirmy, which made her happy. Little kids were supposed to have short attention spans. "But Mom, most of the time I don't remember my nightmares." Then he thought for a second and added, "I'm sorry." The poor kid; he sounded like he really meant it.

"Don't be sorry, sweetie." She petted his hair. "Do your homework. I'll be in the kitchen." She kissed the top of his head before standing up and walking away.

"Mom."

She turned around. He was still sitting cross-legged, staring up at the corner of the ceiling and wringing his hands, a disquieting motion for an eight-year-old boy to be making. It was as if someone else was moving his hands for him. "I remember they were bad," he said. "They almost... hurt."

Annie didn't know what that meant, or what to do about it. She knew it was bad, and that she didn't want Paul to know.

"I'll try to remember next time," he said. "I promise."

She knew she should go back over to him and smooth his hair again, or kiss him or at least touch his face, but instead she just said, "OK, sweetie," and went into the kitchen.

Annie tried to tell herself that it was because she'd done enough already, that maybe he felt smothered and needed some space, that no little boy wants to be constantly kissed and coddled by his mother. But she knew that the real reason she couldn't bring herself to go back over to her son, sitting on the floor, twisted and worrying like an old man, was because the sight of him frightened her.

When Annie had been pregnant and they'd been looking for an apartment, Paul hadn't cared where they were going to live, as long as he could have a room to himself. He would have settled for a neighborhood without great schools, with no decent grocery store within walking distance; he would have lived in Staten Island or Hoboken or East New York. But Annie wouldn't have understood. Living in Hoboken, having to stare down a New Jersey zip code, would have been like admitting defeat; she'd have had to hand in her freethinkers' card for good.

Happily, they'd found their place in Carroll Gardens. It was too expensive, but every place in New York was, and Paul had to admit that he was taken with the obvious charms of the neighborhood. He wasn't above appreciating tree-lined brownstone blocks, and proximity to places that sold coffee with Italian names. He shared all this with Annie, but really, his enthusiasm had nothing to do with the neighborhood. Upstairs, on the opposite side of the hallway from the two larger rooms which would be set aside as their room and the kid's, between the bathroom and the closet, thrown in there like a bored architect's afterthought, was an unclassified room that didn't seem to interest either Annie or the realtor that much. *My study*, Paul had thought, as soon as he saw it. *This is my study*.

The difference between childhood and adulthood, Paul thought, was a question of space. As a child, he and his brother had been forced to share a room until Paul went away to college. *Forced* was the right word: neither of them really minded, but in later years Paul realized the absurdity of sharing in a house which had rooms to spare, which were let out to complete strangers every summer. But they'd accepted it, because they were children, at least for a while, and those were the terms they were presented with. Whatever their parents said life was, that was it.

At Columbia, he lived in the dorms, with a different roommate every year. They lived literally on top of one another, in bunk beds Paul always thought better suited for ten-year-olds than for young men who were supposedly among the nation's intellectual elite. Here, again, he accepted the terms of whoever was in charge, despite their contradictory messages to him about what a privilege it was to attend such a hallowed and respected institution. In the library and in lecture halls, Paul felt a bit of that, but in his room he felt about as respected as a kid at a slumber party.

His senior year, he and his friend Max found an apartment near campus on 108th Street, hoping to find some spatial autonomy at last, to feel like men. But since both of their parents refused to chip in for off-campus housing, they could only afford to split a tiny one-bedroom, with Paul in the living room. It was, if possible, more demeaning than the dorms, especially since they'd both developed sex lives in the intervening years.

Paul had been in New York since then, in a series of shared and non-shared—mostly shared—living situations. When he lived with people, it was all more or less a clown car of too many broke, idealistic people in an apartment designed for one or two rich, settled people. The two times he managed to live alone—a glorified closet in the West Village and a glorified slum on Avenue D—he was paying so much that he couldn't do much more than stay at home.

He'd moved in with Annie after they'd been dating for a year. She lived on East 9th Street, with Eddie, a gay friend of hers from high school. He and Eddie got along well, but found they didn't have anything to talk about when Annie wasn't there, and Paul always felt a self-conscious jealousy that Eddie clearly knew his girlfriend so much better than he did. That was perhaps the most absurd living arrangement yet: he felt like he was playing at adulthood, living with a woman at last, but it was a fake, compromised version; a New York version.

This brownstone, though—this was different. They would live here, Paul decided before they'd even seen the bathroom or the kitchen, and that little room would be his study. His study. He might even make a rule that no one was allowed in there except him. That was acceptable, wasn't it, at least for the kid? "I'm an adult," he'd explain. "This is my space. You won't understand until you're older, and have had to suffer through your own crawlspaces."

He never did make that rule, but there was an unspoken understanding anyway. He didn't know whether his wife and son noticed, but he always made a point of going to the bathroom before he went to his study, so that he could stay there for hours if he wanted to, undisturbed. Then he'd close the door, sometimes lock it, and turn on classical music. Annie never grew to share his love of classical music, despite his best efforts to educate her. It used to bother him, but now he was grateful for the opportunity to have something entirely his own, another indicator that this was *his* space, his, and he shared it with no one.

His sanctum did not, in the end, have quite the cachet he'd originally hoped for; not only did his wife and son not seem to care about being excluded, but he suspected they were grateful for the chance to be alone together. Annie was, anyway; it gave her more time to show Thomas the local vermin or read him scary stories, or whatever other fucked-up secrets she felt inclined to share with their little boy. But he still valued having time to himself, and grudgingly acknowledged that Thomas seemed to enjoy the time he spent with his mother, for some reason.

He sat at an ungracefully stained desk that he'd had since college, the only piece of furniture he'd brought with him from apartment to apartment. Someday, he hoped, it would belong to Thomas, but not until he got the sense that the boy really wanted to use it for something worthwhile. If he became a soap opera actor or a construction worker, Paul would keep it; he'd sat at it for too long, laboring over too many awful love poems, grading too many tests and performing too many longhand lab calculations to let it be used as a storage table.

The pile on the right side of his desk was tall, but neat. Paul knew what everything in it was—primarily notes from old lectures (lectures he'd given, and, deeper in the pile, lectures he'd taken as a grad student). The rest of the desk was more or less neat, if a little dusty, and his laptop rested in the middle, usually closed and sleeping, pushed back from the edge to make room for the papers he was grading.

The wall behind the desk was, top to bottom, a bookshelf. All of Paul's books were here; he didn't keep them anywhere else in the house. This was a departure from what he'd envisioned for himself when he finally had a home of his own; he'd always considered it a priority to display one's books prominently, in public, to send a message to visitors that they were entering the home of a scholar, not to be intellectually outdone or otherwise fucked with. It didn't matter. It was worth it to have all his books in his study, displayed for *him*, every time he looked up. *Good work, Paul,* they seemed to say. *You've conquered this much.* There were a few shelves' worth of what Annie called "science stuff"—college textbooks, reference books, journals. Then Hemingway took up an entire shelf, the prize being the copy of *The Old Man and the Sea* he'd borrowed from the Tuftonboro High School Library and never returned. He liked the Hemingway shelf, and the noir shelf above it—primarily Dashiell Hammett and Raymond Chandler—because they reflected his actual tastes. Much of what was left were books he'd read to impress girls. Some of the stuff he actually liked, most notably Pablo Neruda's love poems, which his sophomore year roommate Steve had encouraged him to buy when he was dating Rita, a comparative lit major, proclaiming them "aphrodisiacs on paper"; others, like the Beat poets, he'd suffered through, motivated only by visions of nymphomaniac librarians trawling Prospect Park for thin, undersexed young men who shared their passion for overrated literature.

To the right of his desk was the end table which held his record player, his record collection lined up underneath. On either side of the turntable were pictures of his family: the first was a black-and-white photo of Annie when she was in college; someone who didn't know better would think it was the display photo that came with the frame, because she looked so posed, holding onto the rope of a big wooden swing, her head cocked at the perfect angle to frame her clean sideways smile, and her long curly hair flying out behind her, a blur of fall foliage in the background.

The other was a picture of Thomas when he was three. Paul had never been much of a photographer, but he was proud of this portrait of his son; he'd managed to capture his essence at an age when that essence wasn't even fully formed yet. It was a close-up, taken from above. Thomas was wearing his blue overalls and a yellow and blue striped shirt, the uniform of timeless childhood that little boys wore in old French movies. His expression, which, on the wrong kind of night, looked almost eerie, was pure Thomas: open, passive, listening. His eyes were wide, but with a control well beyond his years, and his mouth was set and still, giving that impression of inner quiet that still took Paul by surprise in person.

The walls were plastered with maps: New York, Brooklyn, New Hampshire, Paris, the London tube, Europe, South America, and a world map. They provided good fodder for his educational quality time with Thomas, which they had taken to calling Awesome Lessons, a notable exception to the no-kids-allowed-in-the-study rule. It was a great source of pride for him that his son was the best geography student in his third-grade class.

Paul used grading papers as an excuse to be in the study, because it sounded vague but reliably professorial. Really, more often than not he went there to take stock of his possessions, to know that he came from somewhere and had meant something before he ended up here: a husband, a father, a predictable list of discarded ambitions and mediocrity. The books proved it: he knew things. He'd accomplished things. He'd made a significant movement between birth and middle age. Yet all it took was his son asking him a question he couldn't answer to make him feel as if he was standing completely still.

He had been looking at the picture of Thomas for so long that it was beginning to make him uneasy, when he heard that flat, sweet syllable that some years ago had become his name coming from his son's room across the hall.

Annie grew up on the Upper West Side. She'd barely heard of Carroll Gardens as a child, except that everyone knew that the Mafia was there, so it was a safe neighborhood with not a lot else going on. There were still remnants of that past a few blocks south of where they lived, where the F train went underground: red brick apartments with white metal fences and little front yards filled with flowers and statues of the Virgin Mary. On Court Street, old men in newsboy caps would sit on the sidewalk outside Caputo's Bakery and Paisano's Meat Store, speaking Italian and yelling at people they knew across the street. The tiny deli near the subway station that didn't sell much more than garbage bags and cigarettes was still a front for something; it was closed at noon and open at one in the morning, and a reliable cast of old men would march through to the back room, stopping briefly to check the score of the Giants game on the staticky black-and-white TV perched atop the ATM.

Aside from those few blocks, Carroll Gardens had pushed past up-and-coming and was now solidly gentrified. *New York* Magazine called its main drag, Smith Street, Restaurant Row; it was crowded with small, dimly lit trattorias and French restaurants, four different Thai places, an Indian buffet, quirky theme bars with bocce courts or roast-your-own s'mores. There was an upscale comic book store, two independent coffee shops and two Starbucks, and several boutiques, including one that only sold clothes made out of wool and a few that bragged of being "green," a label Annie still didn't entirely understand. Everyone on the street was white, her age or slightly younger, pushing baby strollers or holding the hands of kids about Thomas's age.

To the east was the BQE and the East River; to the west, the area real estate developers had recently given the ambitious name "Gowanus," which referred to the deserted, sewage-smelling industrial streets around the Gowanus Canal; to the north, downtown Brooklyn, a kind of miniature Flatbush Avenue overflowing with discount sneaker stores and Radio Shacks; and to the south, the gray warehouses that eventually ended at Red Hook, whose impressive view of the Statue of Liberty had been recently upstaged by its all-too-vivid viewpoint of the Twin Towers and surround sound proximity to the catastrophe. This part of Brooklyn was like a series of protected kingdoms; beyond each of these borderlands, there was another "real" neighborhood, each one more gentrified than the last. Carroll Gardens was south of Brooklyn Heights and west of Park Slope, where senators and Hollywood actors raised their kids.

Annie knew she had no right, as a New Yorker, to complain about where they lived. Finding a place was impossible, and finding a place suitable for a kid was worse. She liked having restaurants nearby for when they didn't feel like cooking, a coffee shop to sit in when she wanted to get out of the house, bookstores to browse in. Thomas felt a kind of ownership of his favorite stores and restaurants, which she thought was good for a New York kid to have; she liked the idea of him bringing a friend home to visit on a vacation from college and giving them a nostalgic tour about what used to be there, and how it had changed.

Another part of her felt unoriginal for being here, like it was the obvious thing for a kid from the Upper West Side to do once she had a family and didn't know where to go. What if they had found a real *neighborhood*? Somewhere upstate, maybe an hour's commute on the Metro-North, or in the outer reaches of Queens, or even some less offensive part of Connecticut or New Jersey? Or had she made a mistake not going even farther, to the west coast, or even abroad? Paul spoke disapprovingly of the people in his hometown who'd never left, or were even working in the same supermarket where he'd left them when they were teenagers. Just because her home was New York City, did that make it any less sad that she hadn't gone anywhere?

6

On a slow Tuesday, Annie wandered the aisles of Pages bookstore, trying to look busy. She'd always thought that being in charge would mean she wouldn't have to try to look busy anymore, but slow was slow. It was 2pm and she'd run out of things to do.

Her title was Store Manager. She'd only ever worked at this branch of Pages, on 23rd and 6th, known for being one of the franchise's original stores in New York. She'd been promoted to Manager when Thomas was two years old, and thought she had a good shot of being really great at it. She wanted to be the kind of boss that people told about their relationship problems, that they weren't afraid to cry in front of in the break room.

In 1999, Pages expanded to include a Coffee Corner upstairs. They had their own manager, Blake, but he reported to Annie, so she was sort of in charge of the coffee goings-on too. That was when she knew that her Masters in English had been a waste; by then, she'd begun to sense that that was the case already.

She gravitated toward the Coffee Corner on slow days. She didn't want Blake to feel micromanaged, so she avoided hovering there, but now he was on his break. Only one barista, Janae, was working, wiping the pick-up counter. The café was empty.

"Slow!" Annie announced as she approached the counter. Janae looked startled, then confused, then settled into a slightly friendlier version of indifference.

"Yeah. Dead today." She kept wiping the counter. "It was a little busier in the morning, you know, with the coffee-before-work crowd, but..." She shrugged. "Yeah, it's pretty much been like this."

"Are you usually here on Tuesdays, Janae?" Annie felt proud of herself for noticing.

"No, I switched shifts with Larisa, she's coming in tomorrow." After an uncomfortable silence, she offered, "My kid's sick."

"Oh, I'm sorry."

"Yeah. My husband's home with her today but he wants to be careful about taking too many days off. He's a nurse."

This was more information than she'd found out about Janae in the entire time she'd worked here. When had she started—a year ago, a year and a half?

"That was nice of Larisa, to switch with you," she said. "I know sometimes my bookstore folks have a hard time working that out. I always say they can take time off whenever, as long as they find someone to cover their shift, but I guess that's harder than it sounds."

Janae sprayed a fresh cloth and wiped down the nozzles of the espresso machine. She was in her twenties, black, petite, with a taut, curvy figure and a serious expression. She had her braids pulled into a ponytail, and wore a necklace with a gold pendant of a cursive word that Annie couldn't read. Her nails had a striped pink and purple pattern, professionally done.

"Larisa's usually pretty cool about switching with me," she said. "She knows I have a kid, and her kid's old enough to stay home alone now, so it's a little easier for her to leave work."

Annie hadn't known Larisa had a kid either. She wasn't even sure which of the Pages employees were parents.

"How old is your little girl?"

"She's three." Another silence set in, and Janae broke it again. "Her name's Mia." Annie waited for her to say more, but she didn't.

Janae kept cleaning, occasionally sneaking a glance at Annie. Part of her wanted to stay there longer, use this slow day to pump this captive employee for information about everyone, and then start remembering birthdays and asking people about their kids. She would be the best manager any of them had ever had; she would start tomorrow.

The other part of her knew she'd disturbed Janae, not from any particular task, but from solitude, which was more important, really. She felt a natural opening in the conversation to tell Janae about Thomas, but she knew—with a sad, sharp certainty—that Janae did not care that she had a son. The truth was, she didn't care about Janae's daughter either. Not in any way that mattered.

"Hey, Janae, since it's not too busy could you check the fridge in the back and let Blake know if there's anything we need to add to the milk order?"

Janae smiled at her, as if assigning her a menial task had been a merciful act.

"Whenever you have a minute," Annie said. "No rush." She tossed a hand up to wave at Janae as she left and walked back downstairs to her office, bursting with false purpose.

One good thing about work: it wasn't home. Books stood in for the people she lived with. She arranged them alphabetically and made sense of them. The chemistry books were so pleasing to look at, lined up spine to spine, all thick and white. Annie could almost have a conversation with them.

In the children's section, she could imagine her own child running his fingers over the rows of brightly colored cardboard, overwhelmed by his choices, feeling good to be there, to be that age. She pictured him giggling, tugging at her skirt. There was a sitting area with a light blue carpet that she knew would make him feel safe.

Sometimes she didn't want to go home. If it weren't for the way the store looked once it was closed, she might not. Whenever possible, she tried to shove the closing duties onto someone else. She couldn't stand it, that dark walk from her office to the front door, through what should have been familiar territory. The shelves looked suddenly unstable, like they'd grown legs. Everything with some new appendage, and no one had checked with her first. She was the manager of this store. She was supposed to be in charge.

Thomas's school was up towards Atlantic Avenue, on their side of Smith Street. It was almost Brooklyn Heights, a fifteen-minute walk up to the Promenade, one of the places Paul was willing to give New York full, all-hype-deserved credit for. Once the weather got shitty, he'd drive to pick up Thomas at the end of the day, but in September, he could still walk. Today was sunny, cold enough for a sweater but not for a jacket yet; the leaves were about halfway from green to spectacular, and there was an orange hint behind the afternoon daylight. Thomas was usually a good sport about walking home, but when he was uncharacteristically whiny, Paul was not above stopping somewhere on Court Street on the way to silence him with a pastry.

He was early. He recognized other kids from Thomas's class on the playground but didn't see his son; he knew he was around somewhere, probably playing quietly with Ingrid away from the other kids. Paul made his way to the unofficial parents' section, a cluster at the place where the woodchips stopped and the asphalt started that marked the entrance to the playground.

He vaguely recognized the adults, and knew them about as well as he knew any of their kid counterparts. These people, he knew, were probably the most likely candidates for friends, now that he was a father, but he didn't have many friends. Annie didn't either, as far as he knew. He couldn't even really blame that all on having a kid, either; when they were dating, they'd reveled in a giggly me-and-you-against-the-world feeling that makes couples intoxicating to one another and insufferable to other people.

Paul found a spot next to a handsome Indian man whom he recognized as the father of Joshua Varma. The boy was small for his age and had enormous eyes that made him very cute, and at the moment he was maniacally running laps around the swing set, barely avoiding the flying legs of the other kids.

The man saw Paul watching his son, and laughed. "This is not going to end well," he said.

Paul appreciated the guy's nonchalance, and was happy to return it. "Hey, how else are they gonna learn?"

"Exactly. Besides, I want him to get it out of his system now, before he gets home and does anything really destructive around his brother." They watched the little boy run around for another moment before the man extended his hand to Paul. "Ankit."

"Paul," he said. "My son is Thomas." He arched his neck and

scanned the playground. "He's... somewhere. With his friend Ingrid. They're quiet, they kind of keep to themselves."

Ankit looked back at Joshua, who'd recruited another kid to run around the swings with him. "God, that sounds wonderful," he said.

"How old is the little brother?"

"Fourteen months." Ankit shook his head in a way that implied utter exhaustion. Paul didn't entirely buy it; this man looked more well-groomed and put-together than he had in years. "I should give Josh more credit," Ankit continued. "He's actually really great with his brother. Very helpful. He likes feeling responsible, important."

"That's impressive. I was five years older than my brother, and I was completely indifferent to him. I don't know if I ever helped with him at all."

Ankit nodded. "Sure. I know we're lucky, we've talked to other parents who have a big age difference and heard all these horror stories. Kids will absolutely torture each other."

Paul knew that within the confines of polite conversation, he should agree with this so they could move on to some other innocuous subject, but for some reason he couldn't let this inaccuracy rest. "Well... we weren't like that. I really do mean it when I say I was indifferent. We never fought, or even argued, I just kind of didn't have anything to do with him. Even though we shared a room." Ankit was looking at him now. "Still don't," he went on. "We're so different. I guess that's not surprising, huh, given how little we dealt with each other when we were growing up. But yeah, now he's... you know, he kind of floats around, lives somewhere for a while and then moves, usually has some job to make money... I couldn't even tell you where he lives right now. He was in the Bay Area for a while, you know, in California, but I don't know if he's still there." Paul was staring into the distance now, not really directing his comments at anyone in particular. "I haven't actually seen him in years," he said. He was dimly aware of Thomas appearing in his field of vision with Ingrid, walking towards the playground from the far side of the building.

"Is that your son?" Ankit asked, pointing, clearly eager to change the subject. Paul was embarrassed about going off on his tangent, and of all things, about his brother, a subject he never talked about. He nodded and didn't say anything. Thomas and Ingrid edged towards the playground impossibly slowly. They looked so pale and solemn next to the other kids; they might as well have been feral children, appearing from deep in the woods.

"I don't think our kids are friends," Ankit said after a moment, then laughed. "Is that taboo to say?"

It was, and Paul appreciated it. It struck him as a kindness, evening out his own bizarre non-sequitur.

"What do you think," Ankit said, as they watched the kids line up in front of their teacher to go inside and get their things before the day officially ended. "Should we force them to play together?"

Paul really considered it for a moment. Only Ingrid, and no other friends; it had certainly occurred to him that there could be something wrong with that, and he knew Annie didn't even like her, but secretly he thought that was just as weird. Who held a grudge against a little kid?

"Nah," he said. "I think your kid would wear my kid out. And Thomas would probably bore poor Joshua."

"All right." Ankit gave a satisfied nod. "We can tell our wives we gave it a shot."

Paul liked that. He didn't know anything about Ankit's wife; he found himself wondering if she was also Indian, and then immediately felt terrible for thinking it. He glanced over at Ankit instinctively, half-fearing in moments like these that the person next to him could read his thoughts.

"My wife…" Paul said, and wasn't sure where to go from there. "She certainly wishes Thomas had more friends," he concluded.

Ankit nodded again. "My wife worries. So do I, honestly. It's so easy to see anything as a potential warning sign." This time, he was the one directing his words into the ether. "Parenting is scary."

"It is!" Paul felt another surge of speech coming on. "I feel like it's my *job* to be scared for Thomas. But my wife—I don't think she is. She may be scared of *something*, but she's not scared for our son, and it seems to me that anything else is a waste of time at this point. Right? We're parents now. We pretend we're not scared of anything and we use our fear in productive ways, like yelling at our kid not to play too close to the street. Right?"

Ankit stared at him openly this time. *Fuck,* Paul thought. *I did it again. This is why I don't hang out with other parents.*

Their kids arrived, saving them again. Ankit's little boy looked up at Paul curiously as his father said a polite goodbye, and shortly after that, Thomas came up to him, straining under a bulging backpack.

"What have you got in there, rocks?" Paul said.

Thomas hitched it up on his shoulders and didn't smile. "No."

Paul had to laugh at that. *Tough crowd today,* he thought. "All right. Well, good." He took Thomas's hand and they walked south. "Nice day today, isn't it, old pal? I could really use some gelato, how about you?"

7

That night, he peeked into Thomas's room and found him sitting cross-legged on the rug between the bed and the door. It was oval, with a rainbow spiral pattern, one of those innocuous objects that adults take for granted, never stopping to consider if they meet the child's aesthetic sensibilities. If any child had an aesthetic sensibility, Paul was sure, it was this one. He was a little critic, who didn't bite into a chicken nugget without first fixing his features in a discerning frown. Someday he'd get around to asking him what he thought of the rug. It never seemed important enough.

"What are you looking at?" Paul asked, even though it was clear that Thomas was staring into the turtle's tank. He'd meant the question philosophically: what was there to look at in a turtle? They'd offered him a hamster if he wanted one, or even a cat if he promised to help take care of it, but Thomas had been adamant about the turtle. Paul hated the thing; it smelled bad and seemed to mock him, somehow, with the amount of care and energy his son lavished upon it.

"Alexander looks hungry," Thomas said without looking up.

"We fed him earlier."

"I know," the boy said, looking up, "but—"

"Unless I'm losing my mind." Paul knelt down so that he was crouching beside Thomas. "Which is always possible." His son remained staring into the small gray world, as if it were fascinating. There was a patch of grass in one corner, a water bowl in the other, and a trail of poop between the two.

Thomas didn't laugh. "I know," he said, "but he's looking at me like he wants something."

He wanted to laugh at that, or say *I know the feeling*. "He's a turtle," he said, moving his face closer to Thomas's, trying to tease out a reaction. "He probably wants to be more like you."

He might as well have said nothing. Thomas was transfixed by the little dinosaur the way other children his age were hypnotized by television, an artifact that he pretty much ignored. "Yeah," he breathed, the word stretching itself out into territory where it lost its meaning. Inside the tank, Alexander moved one leg forward with deliberation, like an old man doing Tai Chi in a park.

Paul knew that only a poor comedian had to explain his jokes, but he refused to lose to a reptile in the battle for his son's attention. "He's thinking, *Damn! I forgot to be born a human.*"

Finally, Thomas looked back at him, with a breaking patience that reminded Paul of being five or six years old and asking his mother to watch him while he jumped off the dock into the lake. "Dad," he said. *I am looking, Paul*, she'd say, before returning to her newspaper, or sometimes simply, *Not now, Paul.*

He'd received that withering look from his son a lot lately. It had happened that Saturday, when they'd taken the subway to Manhattan to meet Annie for lunch. It was a crowded train, and they were standing by the door, Paul holding the pole and Thomas holding his hand.

At one point, Thomas tugged on his hand and asked, "What's that noise?"

Paul listened and tried to hear, he really did, but nothing unusual rose to the surface of the clacking landscape. "That's the noise of mass transit," he said. He'd thought it was a pretty clever answer.

"No," Thomas said, "I know what the subway sounds like. I mean *that* noise."

Since he'd become a father, Paul had discovered that his lifelong flaw of taking failed jokes too personally had only worsened when the unimpressed audience was his own kid.

"Thomas," he said, "when you say, 'What's that noise?' in a place that's very noisy, it's not very helpful to the person you're asking. It's like going to the middle of Times Square and saying, 'Hey, who's that guy?'"

Next to them, one of those Remnants of Old New York ladies glared at him, pursed her lips and moved her shoulders up and down. Well, what the hell does she know, he thought. She thought she could dish out disapproval and remain impervious to it because of her tailored peacoat from Bloomingdale's, her face that miraculously resisted the effects of probably fifty-some years of heavy makeup, her dainty Minnie Mouse gloves, pearl earrings, latest issue of the *New Yorker*, her century's worth of knowledge of the city block for block, what had been where and when and just how much everything had gone to hell, with no thought of ever leaving because, Paul and the rest of the world knew, the truth was, she wouldn't survive anywhere else. This was supposed to be the city where outsiders get eaten alive, but the cruel joke was that really, it was just a breeding ground for frightened insiders, people like this woman, who would never be able to set foot anywhere else without turning into stone and cracking all the way down.

"OK," Thomas said, "but there's a weird noise. Listen."

Paul ground his teeth. He was being challenged. The lady in the peacoat knew it too. He hated her. He hated everyone on the subway in this moment; they might not all be showing it as brazenly as her, but he knew every single one of them walked around the world feeling entitled to think, even to say openly, that they were from the greatest place on Earth. Everyone he'd met here had that cockiness, to some degree, like you should be impressed by their very existence.

"Thomas," he said, invoking the boy's name as a reminder to the woman, and anyone else who might be listening, that he was the boy's father, and had some ownership of him that was not to be questioned.

"You're not listening," Thomas said.

Paul moved his thumb over the back of Thomas's palm with what he hoped felt like affection. "I am listening, old pal," he said as gently as he could. "Sounds distinctly like the Queens-bound F train."

"Dad—"

"Next stop, East Broadway."

"Dad."

"Stand clear of the closing doors, please."

"Fine, Dad, forget it."

"Ding-dong."

Now Thomas was quiet. The old lady had gone back to her *New Yorker*; at least one battle had been won.

After a moment, so quietly that Paul almost didn't hear him, Thomas said, "It's gone now."

"Glad to hear it," Paul said, patting his son's hand without looking at him.

"Yeah," he heard that familiar somber voice say somewhere below him. "Never mind."

Now, Thomas turned back to Alexander's tank. "Sometimes I hear him moving around at night," he said. "And I don't like that, so if he's hungry I want to feed him now, so he'll be able to sleep."

"He moves around, huh? Does that keep you up?" Paul looked at the turtle as if he might provide some answers. The shell was beautiful, sure, Paul could see that, but everything else was unpleasant. The face, which is supposed to be the repository for expression in living things, was just a collection of brownish lines, like a piece of food that had been left out too long.

"No, it doesn't keep me up, I just don't like it." He paused a moment, then added, "Hearing him." There was something wounded in his voice, a new thing Paul didn't recognize.

"Why?" He placed his hand on his son's shoulder. "You know it's just him in there, that there's nothing to be afraid of."

"I know that," Thomas said, his body stiff under his hand. "I just don't like it."

"The only thing we have to fear is fear itself. FDR said that. Remember I told you about him?"

In one motion, Thomas moved out from under his father's grip and turned to face him. Again Paul thought of his mother, sitting by the lake. There was a narrowed intensity in the boy's eyes that went beyond everyday annoyance; his stare seemed to be asking, *Why?* The question Paul had hated coming up against his whole life, until he was a father and could answer it with cool, straightforward answers that couldn't be argued with: because of atmospheric pressure, because there's a thing called a term limit, because Brooklyn used to be considered a separate city from Manhattan. This was a different *why*, more personal, less forgiving: Why are you doing this? Why are you the way you are? Why can't you just leave me alone?

Then Thomas said it out loud.

"I don't know why you're talking about that stuff. I was just saying that Alexander looks hungry."

Not now, Paul, his mother would say, when he'd called up the nerve to approach her for whatever it was. *I'm busy.* He'd stay in the doorway and never get too close. The greater the distance, the more clearly her message came through.

Paul stood up. "Let me see if Mom has any carrot peels she can spare," he said, then waited a moment for Thomas to thank him. He didn't; he was watching the tank as if it held a secret Paul couldn't possibly understand.

On a hot autumn night in 1981, David Stellar walked to the kitchen of his Scottsdale home, took a knife from the drawer, walked back upstairs to where his wife was sleeping, and stabbed her twenty-six times. He was asleep the entire time.

Paul knew that Stellar was acquitted for reasons of temporary insanity. He knew that Stellar's mother and sister told the police that he had never walked in his sleep as a child, and that he and his wife had, by all accounts, a peaceful marriage. He knew about others, too. The woman in London who strangled her toddler; the woman who found her husband's .380 Bersa in a hallway closet and shot him twice in the chest; the man who dragged his wife out of bed to beat her to death. All asleep. Their verdicts were varied and controversial; trials overflowed with character witnesses who swore up and down they couldn't imagine anyone less likely to commit such atrocities.

He read about each case multiple times, looking for something that he knew wasn't there, some pearl of wisdom to be gleaned, a moral tacked on the end: to avoid being a victim yourself, follow these simple steps. But he knew these were matters of record, not advice. Paul wondered how many other people had come to these websites, like him, for some backward form of solace. Probably none—these were designed for people like his aunt Grace, whose shelves were filled with fat true crime paperbacks. To those people, his deepest fears were entertainment.

As he became a scholar of somnambulism-related deaths, he kept his eye out for accounts of near-misses, but couldn't find any, which led him to believe that all of those people had somehow extricated themselves from the situation and hadn't had any desire to relive it. He wondered if that was a sign that he should take some kind of drastic action, but, as with everything else in his life recently, he had no idea how to proceed.

His need to research this, to dig deeper and deeper into the Internet until he had a satisfactory answer, had started when they came back from France and gone on to become an obsession. He couldn't go a full day at work without indulging the habit, and at home, it was becoming more and more difficult to walk by his study without going in, opening his laptop, and disappearing into more gruesome cautionary tales.

When he'd sat with his wife and son and watched the towers fall, he'd had the overwhelming feeling that they weren't safe anymore; that there was nowhere they could go that would be safe, and that life held no guarantees. He'd only realized then that he was an idiot—he'd actually been living his life up to that point like a child, completely certain that there *were* guarantees. The attacks were, in a way, a blow to his ego—retribution for having the audacity to become so smug.

At least I have these people, he'd thought as he'd kissed the top of Thomas's head after tucking him in that night, and later, in bed, as he and Annie clung to each other as if that were the only way to make anything make sense. This is what people do: they use each other as shields against other horrors. This was how to get through the next day, and the days after that: the outside world was dangerous, but here it was safe.

He would rise to the demands of being a father in the wake of a tragedy: raise his child carefully, be willing to answer his questions honestly, and always reassure him that he was safe, no matter what he saw on TV. With them, he was safe.

A few months later, he was slapped back to reality again, when Annie started sleepwalking. Apparently, the floor beneath their feet in their own house wasn't steady, either. Maybe the only honest thing to say to Thomas was, "I love you, but I can't keep you safe."

8

They'd bought him Alexander as an apology for fighting. Thomas knew that was how things worked. Ingrid's parents bought her cat Fraidy for her on a Thursday, and on Saturday they told her they were getting divorced. She invited him over to meet the cat and told him she'd known the divorce was coming, because they'd been fighting.

Ingrid didn't seem upset or anything, which made Thomas wonder if divorce was really as bad as everyone said it was. She looked pretty peaceful, actually, with her hands folded in her lap, sitting on the edge of her bed, just sort of watching Thomas pet Fraidy. Her head was cocked just like the cat's. Someone who didn't know Ingrid might think that she was trying to imitate it, but Thomas knew that really, Fraidy was imitating her. Ingrid always sat lopsided like that; it lifted one side of her hair up off her shoulder so the other side hung down lower. She looked all right like this, Thomas thought. Like herself.

"My parents fight," Thomas said, then felt a little bad because he wondered if he was supposed to ask her how she was feeling or something like that.

But Ingrid hadn't minded. That was the nice thing about her. She let Thomas say the things he thought about, as he thought them. Other people, adults and kids, sometimes gave him this look like they wished he'd rearrange the things in his head before he let them come out of his mouth. He was used to it by now, and he'd gotten better at saying things in an order that people would like better. But every once in a while, it was nice to talk to Ingrid, who let him speak the way his brain wanted to.

"How long have they been fighting?" she asked.

Thomas wasn't sure what that meant. His parents had always had little arguments, just about every night, since always. But that was normal, wasn't it? Were there people whose parents *didn't* have those arguments? How did they know who should pick the kid up at school, or go get milk when they ran out?

"It was really bad this summer," Thomas said, and Ingrid nodded. He meant in France. On the first day of school, when she'd asked him how the trip was, he'd told her it was interesting and sort of OK.

She didn't say anything, and Thomas knew that meant she was waiting for him to tell her the rest. They'd been friends since they were five and they'd always told each other everything. He'd never felt worried about it the way he did now.

Most of the time, Ingrid looked the way they'd overheard her dad describe her at a dinner party: "Serious, quiet and sharp." They'd spent a long time trying to figure out what that might mean.

"Sharp means smart," Thomas said, "I think."

"Well," said Ingrid, "I am smart."

"Yeah, you are. And quiet, I guess."

"Sometimes."

"And, what was the other one?"

"Serious."

Thomas thought about that one. He tried to really think about it. "Serious?"

Ingrid shrugged.

"I don't think you're really serious. I mean—do you feel serious?"

Ingrid looked up and moved her eyes from side to side, a tiny bit at a time. Thomas could tell she was moving the word around in her brain, the way he had. "I feel serious," she said.

But she never looked that serious to him, because of the little smile on the side of her face that never really went anywhere, even when they were talking about stuff like parents fighting.

It was a good smile, a friendly one, and it usually made him want to talk to her about whatever it was that he wanted to talk about, but he was having a hard time getting the words out about the fighting in France. He didn't really understand it, and when he talked to people, especially to Ingrid, he liked to understand what he was talking about. His dad never talked about anything without knowing everything there was to know about it. Thomas liked that; he thought it was a good way to go.

What happened was, his parents had been fighting a lot, everywhere they went. Last summer, after second grade, after that year when all the 9/11 stuff happened, they'd traveled in a rental car all over France. His dad had mapped everything out. He'd even let Thomas help him, sort of; he remembered sitting on the floor of his dad's study with the green Michelin maps spread out in front of him, listening to his father's voice and tracing his finger along from town to town. "It's just words right now, old pal," his dad had said, "weird-looking words that we don't understand. But soon we'll really *be* there. Think about that. We'll be right there!" Then he'd put his finger on top of Thomas's, next to an E somewhere on the left side of the map.

His dad kept asking him if he was scared about flying. Thomas couldn't figure out if he meant because he'd never flown before or because of the 9/11 stuff. Either way, he wasn't scared; his dad had told him that flying was the safest form of travel, and a bunch of numbers about how many people die in cars each year and how many die in airplanes, which was way less. He didn't get why he'd told him all that stuff and then still worried about him being afraid of flying. He didn't tell his dad this part, but it had made him a little scared about riding in the car, which he hadn't been before.

Thomas had never been to the airport before. He hadn't known it was going to be so huge and crowded, that there were so many people going places on planes. They had to do a million things before they could get on the plane, and his parents kept complaining about all of it and saying how different it was, and talking about 9/11. Thomas didn't really understand what 9/11 had to do with them waiting around at the airport, but they both seemed so annoyed by whatever it was that he didn't want to ask.

After they'd stood in a line and then another line and gotten bagels and walked a really long way, past a bunch of signs that said the same things over and over, they finally came to a hallway with a bright blue carpet and a lot of chairs, and his dad told him it was the very last place they had to be before they got on the plane.

"Our plane's gonna pull up right there, Thomas," he said, pointing out the big window that took up a whole wall. "You want to go look out at the planes taking off and landing?"

Thomas didn't know why, but he really didn't. His dad said it like it would be a really fun thing to do, and Thomas had really been sure, this whole time, all through the airport and the lines and all the 9/11 talk, that he still wasn't scared about flying, but now, seeing them up close… he wasn't scared, exactly, but he didn't want to go look at them taking off and landing. He knew that for sure. He didn't even really like being able to see them up close through the big windows. He found a seat facing away from the window and sat there with his mom and read one of the books he'd brought in his backpack while they waited. When they walked up to the tunnel that took them onto the plane, he made sure not to look out the window.

A lot of the trip was actually pretty fun. Thomas liked the French people they met; all the waiters and the owners of the bed and breakfasts were nice and seemed to think he was cute, but not in that annoying way most adults had. They seemed to think he was interesting, too, and that's what he wanted to be.

His parents didn't seem happy, though. Sometimes he'd lose them for a moment, walk a little behind or a little ahead of them and when he ran to catch up or turned around to wait for them, they'd be frowning at each other and talking quickly and quietly in that dangerous way grown-ups speak when something's serious. It was a language he didn't understand, and didn't want to, and hoped he'd never have to.

Usually he didn't hear exactly what they were saying, but sometimes he caught a couple words—"no chance"; "you seem to think"; "how will he ever". He didn't even remember who had said what. Once, in the car, there was a long fight about the way they both spoke French. Thomas hated that one, because it started out as a nice conversation. He remembered that his parents were making fun of each other in that funny way they had, and he was listening to both of them and giggling in the back seat and they were driving past huge sunflower fields that looked like someone had drawn them with a fat yellow crayon and everything seemed OK, like all the stupid and annoying stuff hadn't been real and he was just now waking up in the real vacation—and then, without anyone telling him, he knew he had to stop laughing, that it wasn't funny anymore. He didn't know why or what either of them had said to make it that way, but it was over, and there weren't any more nice moments after that.

That was the night his mom and dad stopped talking by the end of dinner. Something happened so fast he didn't see it, and by the time they were driving back to their bed and breakfast, the car was silent. When they got there, his dad told him to go inside, and a minute later, his mom came inside, but his dad wasn't there.

His mom didn't say anything when she came in. She didn't tell him what to do. Thomas knew that adults were supposed to tell him what to do, pretty much all the time. When that didn't happen, he did a lot of waiting. He stayed by the door, like he wasn't allowed to come in any further until she said so. He felt as if his feet were glued there. At that moment, he would have put all his clothes on backwards, if she'd told him to, or gone out into the night and run around the streets of the little French town. He would have done anything, if she would just have told him what to do.

But she didn't even look at him; he was right there by the door, and maybe if he had left she wouldn't even have noticed. She moved around the room like she didn't know him, like she was just a woman on vacation by herself. She took her shirt off and pulled her night-gown on, slipped her pants off underneath, sat on the edge of the bed and ran a brush through her hair. She was facing away from him, so Thomas couldn't tell what she was looking at, or if she was looking at anything.

She still hadn't said anything to him, hadn't even looked at him, when she lifted her legs and swung them under the covers. Thomas thought it was a funny way to get into bed; he realized he'd probably never seen his mother get into bed before. When would he? They were all living together now, for these three weeks, like those poor families in the old days where everyone shared a room, the parents and the kids and the pets and everybody. Thomas wondered if that was nice sometimes, for those families, or if they were always sad about being so poor.

The place they were staying was like a cottage, surrounded by other cottages and the big stone house where the owners lived and cooked the food. Thomas liked it. In the mornings, they'd eat breakfast outside, in the courtyard that the cottages faced. Inside, there was Thomas's small bed on one wall, the television on the other, and his parents' bed between the two, but further back, in front of the bathroom door. Thomas kept watching from the door, which seemed like a hundred miles away from the bed, waiting for something to change. For a while, nothing did. She was completely under the covers, a long lump dressed up in sheets.

He didn't want to think of it right then, so he tried hard to push it out of his brain, but in the end his brain won: *She's a monster under there.*

It didn't seem fair to remember that right then; he knew there were times when he forgot about monsters, like when the three of them were having a good time. When he was little, he hadn't even figured it out yet; couldn't his brain pretend not to know again? The thing was, he loved his mother then, so much it didn't make sense, like parents and kids in movies who can't stop crying while they hug each other. But he couldn't hug her. He couldn't even go near her. The back he was seeing was the back of a monster; under the sheets, she had scales and claws. She had sharp teeth and yellow eyes.

Then he heard a noise. It was so horrible and so surprising that it made his shoulders jerk back. The monster, his mom, was crying. Thomas had heard other people cry, but she sounded different, like an animal, whining like it needed food. Then the whining sort of opened up and she sounded like something breaking, like when you fall down and your arm twists in a way it's not supposed to.

"Mom?" he asked, less to speak to her than to know that he was still there. It was one of those tricks you use in a dream to wake yourself; Thomas hoped it might work and he'd wake up in the back of the car, with his forehead against the window and the sunflowers zipping by outside. But nothing changed, and his mom didn't say anything.

He stayed where he was. It felt like a long time. At some point he remembered that his father wasn't there and realized that he had no idea where he was. He knew he was probably a monster, or that maybe he'd disappeared, but all he could think of was that they were on another continent; his dad could literally be anywhere in the world. All he knew was that he wasn't there.

54

Then his mom talked. The crying didn't stop, just sort of shifted and made room for her voice to squeeze through, high and wobbly. "Thomas," she said. "I'm sorry. Why don't you just go to bed now, OK?"

"Where's Dad?"

Her crying shook back and forth like it was getting pushed around by the wind. "I don't know," she said, "but let's not worry about it. Let's go to bed now."

He didn't feel like sleeping. He didn't feel like anything close to sleeping, but she'd asked him to, and she was crying. Thomas was sure there must be a rule about having to do what a monster asks, no matter what. He was pretty sure a sad monster would become the angriest kind of monster, too.

Thomas got into bed without doing anything else. She hadn't asked him to brush his teeth or wash his face, so even though he knew he was supposed to, he didn't. He hid under the covers and changed into his pajamas, the way he always did when they were all staying in the same room on vacation, then ducked into the bed and pulled the blankets up to his chin. Sometimes that helped when he couldn't sleep, making himself as warm and snug as possible; a blanket monster, like his mom was now.

It didn't work this time, because the blanket was gray and scratchy. There were things he didn't like about France—no one seemed to care about making things soft, or fun to look at. Where was his dad?

Sometimes, Thomas remembered, thinking something over and over again made him sleepy. He closed his eyes and rubbed the blanket against his chin until it almost didn't feel scratchy anymore and thought, *Where's Dad? Where's Dad?*

After a while, it worked. He fell asleep.

He wanted to tell Ingrid the whole story, about what happened after he fell asleep that night, but he couldn't. It would come out sounding sadder than he wanted it to, and he might even start crying. He wasn't sure, though. Thomas didn't like when he didn't know what was going to happen.

Ingrid was smiling and waiting. She waited so well. Sometimes he wondered whether that meant she was stupid; that's what some kids at school said. It didn't really make any sense to him, because he always thought Ingrid was one of the smartest people he knew, almost as smart as his dad in a weird way, but the kids at school knew about a lot of stuff that he didn't. Sometimes he thought maybe he should just trust them.

He shook his head and said, "It was really bad."

Ingrid nodded. She looked like what he'd just said was really important. "And then you got Alexander," she said.

9

"I hate that fucking turtle," Paul said as he entered the kitchen. He wasn't trying to make conversation; it was all he could think about. He wanted to start an argument about whose idea it had been and who had let it happen.

Paul took stock of his wife. She was leaning against the counter and watching the tea kettle with that wan look she'd acquired recently, and she was already in the nightgown, the graying gauzy thing that announced to him that, at eight thirty in the evening, she'd given up. Paul had never thought of Annie as thin; she'd always been hearty and robust, words you'd use to describe a good meal. When he pictured a rough sketch of her, what rose to the surface was her round moon face, and the smile that anchored it. He didn't like this new figure, slim in an old-fashioned, unappealing way, a haven't-you-eaten way. Her hips were fading, her breasts becoming shallow slopes, shrugging off roundness as if they didn't need it anymore.

Annie didn't say anything. He knew she hated the turtle, too. It was hard not to—his existence in their home had come about for lack of a better idea. And now that it was here, it wasn't working.

"Thomas loves him," she said with her back to him. "That's what matters, don't you think?"

Where, Paul wondered, had she inherited this passive-aggressive gene? That was supposed to be the realm of his parents, a New England mainstay. Annie, the self-proclaimed assertive New York Jew, was supposed to be in-your-face with her accusations and insults. "If your mother hates me so much," she had said once on the way back from a Christmas vacation in Tuftonboro, Thomas in the back seat, soaking up every word, "I wish she would just say it." It had been hard to take, coming from her, queen of double meanings, of well-crafted backward verbal stabs and eye rolls.

"I don't know if 'love' is the right word," Paul said. "He's found something to fixate upon." He ignored her pointed sigh and added, "I suppose that's something."

"Do you want something?" she asked, turning around. When they'd met, her face was beginning to form smile lines. Now, her mouth, when at rest, formed the shape of a frown the way a child would draw it, a perfect upside-down U.

"The thing is hungry. The turtle. Do you have any vegetable peels?"

Wordlessly, she walked to the garbage can under the kitchen table, pulled off the lid, and began to move her hands around inside it.

It was infuriating and sad and fascinating to watch. He hadn't asked her to dig through the garbage; she could have said, "No, I already threw them out," and left it at that, but here she was, with her hands caked in layers of God knows what in a display of... what? Sacrifice? Was he supposed to thank her?

"Hey," he said. "Have you given any more thought to that thing we talked about?"

"About seeing a shrink?" Her ass, flat and shiny in the silk, moved slightly from side to side as the rest of her rummaged in the garbage. "Not really. I told you I'd revisit that if the sleepwalking got to a point I was really worried about."

"Well..." He waited for her to face him, which, after some more dramatics in the garbage can, she did. "Look, Annie, I want you to take this seriously. I've been patient, but, if you don't see someone and show me you're going to take care of this, then—"

"Then what? You'll divorce me? Is this a threat?"

He didn't look at her. "After what happened in France, I don't think it's that unreasonable," he said, so quietly he wasn't sure she could hear him.

It felt like a low blow to invoke that idiotic disaster of a trip, which Paul knew was primarily his fault. In the early spring of 2002, fed up with the cacophony of patriotism, determined to get on an airplane somehow in defiance of the paranoia and fearmongering, and desperately needing a vacation anyway, as their home grew tenser by the minute, he'd bought tickets on a whim, manically, without consulting her.

He'd managed to get her on board pretty easily. They could afford it if they traveled on the cheap, which Paul was only too happy to research and plan, and post-9/11 panic had driven airplane ticket prices down already. He knew she'd been to Paris or Rome or somewhere with some ex-boyfriend and longed for another trip like that; the farthest he'd gone with her was California, once, before Thomas was born, and since then they didn't venture much further than upstate or to New Hampshire to see his family. He also knew she'd get some irritating New Yorker satisfaction from being the mother of a child who'd been to Europe before age ten.

Imagining the trip's potential together had been fun. They'd gotten into the planning together, involved Thomas, obsessed over details. Three, four months before it happened, the vacation had been imbued with redemptive powers. By the time July came, it was as if they were embarking on a religious pilgrimage.

Of course it was a catastrophe, Paul remembered thinking on the plane ride home, out a couple thousand dollars, staring out the window, barely interacting with his wife or son. Of course.

"It's still happening, Annie," he said now, trying to sound gentle. "It hasn't gone away."

Then he noticed the carrot skins. They were slimy and grayish-brown, hanging off her arm like seaweed pried off a shipwreck. It was hard to imagine they'd come from a healthy living thing. He felt cruel, as if he had deliberately chosen to do this at the most humiliating moment possible.

She made no motion to clean herself up. "I'll see someone," she said. "I'll find a name tomorrow, and I'll go."

When she looked up, she held the skins out to him, like a sacrificial offering. He didn't want to touch them, but he did; held his hand underneath hers and allowed her to let the long, wet strands slip through her fingers and onto his waiting palm. "Thank you," he said, and went upstairs to feed the turtle.

That night, Annie went for a walk around the house in her dreams. She knew she was dreaming, but she couldn't wake up.

In the dream, the house was dark and silent. She ran her hands over every surface, like she was trying to find something. No one was there except her, and, it seemed in the dream, no one else had ever lived there.

She kept waiting for the feeling, something to tell her that when she woke up she'd be somewhere else. She was beginning to like the feeling, rather than fear it. It felt like something was looking out for her. It was a treat, in a way, never knowing where she would wake up—maybe one night she'd walk all the way into a new house, a new life. Everything that came before would be a dream. People would laugh when she told them about it.

She woke up in bed. Paul was asleep next to her. She flexed her toes under the covers, wide awake.

10

She shut herself in her office and typed "sleep disorder specialists" into the search engine.

Sleep disorder. Whoever invented the names for these things was either cruel and self-satisfied, or a recovered victim who was smug about their success. Some people are unable to perform the basic functions living things need to stay alive. You don't need two working kidneys or an appendix, but sleep—that's non-negotiable. And she couldn't do it right.

A list of doctors popped up on her screen, that familiar arrangement of bigger and smaller letters, names which looked important by virtue of the fact that they were there, on the screen—instant authority. She was a sucker. She'd fall for anything. She'd listen to some quack and become one of those stories you hear about, some poor woman who goes to a "doctor's office" in a one-room apartment over a garage in Queens and never comes out again.

She couldn't do it yet. Not yet. She put her cursor back in the search box and deleted the words as if the letters were trying to get away from her. She watched the word disappear: t, then s, then i—*special. Sleep disorders special.* She liked the way that looked. She kept deleting, then pressed Enter.

Her computer spat up a list: Sleep Disorders. She spent what seemed like her entire day there, reading about problems she didn't have.

Apparently, in another universe, she could have had restless legs. Legs that won't stop moving, even as the body attempts to sleep. Somewhere, she told herself, a woman was sitting in front of a computer screen and feeling cold air on her wet cheeks, thinking about her restless legs, stirring and stirring in the night as her husband slept beside her, his legs quiet as logs, as babies, as babies clinging to logs, floating on a gentle dream river. They were tearing her life apart, these jumpy legs. They were ruining her marriage. Her husband thought, not so secretly, that she was a freak. Who could possibly lose the ability to simply lie still? This woman felt that there was something desperately, fundamentally wrong with her.

Annie read for hours, about sleep apnea, insomnia, night terrors. She ignored anything she found about sleepwalking, telling herself that those were questions she could ask the doctor, and making no effort to find a doctor.

Annie knew she had a right to be outraged at her husband's setting terms and issuing ultimatums; but it wasn't that, exactly.

She'd spent several failed relationships trying to keep up with men who were, in some imperfect sense of the word, more *interesting* than her—artists and poets and musicians, who lived in crumbling lofts and half-assed their way through day jobs, whose friends seemed bored with her, who'd read more than her and barely disguised their resentment about it. This was, Annie understood well into her twenties, what romance was: an intellectual challenge, an exhausting gauntlet of having to prove herself with an occasional intimate reward after the gallery opening ended and everyone else went home for the night. To find a well-groomed, irony-free man attractive was a form of sexual deviancy.

When she met Paul, it was a month or two after her relationship with David, the photographer, ended. In retrospect, there was probably more to it, but at twenty-seven she summed up the breakup as: she didn't look as good naked as his favorite model, Cynthia, and hadn't read as much Sontag.

She'd never actually met anyone like Paul before, just seen them around her on the subway on their way to mysterious white-collar jobs in suits and ties, a bygone era of men rounding out the New York wallpaper. She was intrigued by the optics of him, excited by the opportunity to shun the Davids of her past by fearlessly embracing an honest-to-goodness square.

They met for coffee at a diner near campus that wasn't trying to be anything other than what it was. Its colors were ugly but earnest, and its staff were old ladies, Brooklyn lifers. Paul was surprised when she said she'd never been here before. "It's right across the street," he said.

She imagined him going through each day making decisions that easily, without forethought or intention, without pondering aesthetics or atmosphere. She smiled at him.

On that first date, he told her about going with a friend to see *Contempt* at the Film Forum. "Have you seen it? It's French."

"Yes. A few times, actually."

"A *few* times?" He grimaced. "Maybe I shouldn't tell this story."

"Tell it!"

"OK, OK." He'd put down his triple decker egg salad sandwich and splayed his hands out on either side of the plate, like he needed to fully gather his thoughts. "So, OK, I did not understand that movie at all. Not at all. If you gave me a million dollars, I couldn't tell you what it was about."

She'd never heard anyone speak that way about a movie. About almost anything. Especially not a man. He didn't look like he was trying to make a joke—he looked, in fact, almost distressed, truly asking for help—but she laughed.

"I'm serious!" he said. "Can you tell me what it's about?"

That made her laugh more. Something about this guy in a button-down shirt with a half-eaten egg salad sandwich (which he'd ordered halfway through the date, declaring, "I'm sorry, I honestly didn't think I'd be hungry but I am"), pleading at her across the table with huge eyes to explain a movie all her friends thought was brilliant, made her laugh hysterically. It was wobbly and uncontrolled; she hadn't laughed that way in a long time. Something warm and giddy rose in her chest, something that felt a lot like relief. She tried to stop, because she was genuinely self-conscious and her cheeks were getting hot, but he kept saying things that made her laugh more.

"I really hated it," he said, as she was on the verge of regaining composure, "I'm sorry," which made her start laughing again. He didn't seem offended or embarrassed; he actually seemed to enjoy the sight of her in hysterics, and watched patiently, with a small smile.

"Don't be sorry, don't be sorry," she said when she'd finally pulled herself together, wiping tears from her eyes. "Do you really want me to explain it to you? Or, what I think it's about, anyway?"

"Please." He eagerly resumed the egg salad, staring at her as he ate as if he were about to receive some profound and elusive truth.

"Well..." she cleared her throat involuntarily. "It's about, well, a few things. It's about this deteriorating relationship and how that kind of resentment can build over time, and it's also about film, I mean, the medium of film and how it's used to tell a story like this, and, uh..." She felt herself tightening up again. She was sure she sounded like an idiot. "The... well, there's the film we're watching, and in the film we're watching they're trying to make a film version of *The Odyssey*, right, and—"

"They were?"

She looked at him out of the corner of her eye, assuming he was joking. Again, his giant, earnest eyes told her he wasn't.

"I'm completely serious," he said. "I missed that entirely."

She felt herself beginning to crack up again.

"*The Odyssey*?" he said. "Are you sure?"

She held it together for a moment, not wanting to seem unkind. "Well, yeah. Don't you remember all those Greek statues in the scenes where they're filming? What did you think those were about?"

At this, Paul threw his hands in the air and sat back in the booth. "I really don't know. I thought they were a symbol for something."

Now they were both laughing. "A symbol for what?"

He shook his head. "I really hadn't thought it out that far."

Everything after that felt natural, a path of no resistance. They saw each other again less than a week later, slept together after the second date, and more or less became inseparable. The feeling of that first date stayed with her for a long time—years, maybe. She didn't have to try anymore. She was finally interesting enough. It was as if Paul had never met anyone like the people she used to associate with before him, like she was the first woman with any opinions or any darkness. He made her feel exotic, dazzling, exciting, like the East Village boys she'd trailed behind for so long, feeling like nothing special. Paul saw her weirdness and loved it and protected it, because in some ways it was just for him. She loved him for that, and—this was an idea that had never really occurred to her before—she loved herself, too.

Then, slowly but unmistakably, life had ironed itself out into mundanities, expectations lowered. She knew she couldn't be dazzling to a husband the way she could to a boyfriend; it wasn't sustainable. It was an old story, she knew, that happened to everyone, kids and commutes and budgets and big and small tragedies. Sometimes she wondered if the people of her early twenties, David and his models and all the beautiful women and men draped all over the lower half of Manhattan and the boroughs, had managed to avoid drudgery, if they'd maintained their breakneck pace off the boring beaten path, or if they, too, had run out of parties and drugs and avant-garde fashions and now were just like her, reasonably dressed and hauling a routine back and forth on the subway each day.

She knew it was inevitable that Paul wouldn't find her a quirky novelty forever. Still, she wished she'd been able to transcend the inevitability.

Then, that spring, she'd been given a gift. Some part of her had woken up, and she was no longer just an average wife. There was a heaviness to this particular development, sure, a potential danger; but that was life, Annie thought: you get older, and your quirks can't all be cute anymore. This was an adult's quirk. Most wives slept through the night, but she was special.

But he didn't think so. He didn't love that part of her anymore; he wanted to kill it.

And no fucking way was she going to let him do that.

Paul thought about other women, of course. They weren't pipe dreams, either; they were women his age. Paul wasn't attracted to any of his students. They were just too ridiculous for him, the twenty-year-olds who threw their youth and their sex around like they were getting away with something.

But there was Kathy Burke, for example, the anthropology professor whose office was two doors down from his, with her solid shoulders and wide stance, like she had been made to work the earth and made a wrong turn into academia. She dressed with embarrassing conservatism, her wardrobe a beige amalgam of wool and tweed from the 1950s schoolteacher collection. But from the neck up she was Janis Joplin, with a thick mane of mermaid hair and smile lines around her eyes, and there was something about the way she'd laughed the first time he'd mistakenly referred to her as "Professor Burke" that made her next words, "Call me Kathy," sound sweet and familiar, like he'd been waiting for them.

His elaborate fantasies about Kathy often involved his desk. Her office was a mysterious forbidden place he'd never seen, and every time he tried to place them there it felt too dirty, like he was sullying her, in spite of all the things he'd already done to her in his mind.

They'd cross paths at the copy machine. Kathy talked about the weather and made bad jokes—"I thought it would be summer by the time I got here, it took me so damn long to get out here this morning. I thought I'd moved into a new hemisphere"—and it was all so lovable, the way she had no idea that as he nodded dumbly at her, he was imagining shoving one hand straight down the front of her blouse, yanking it out from where it was tucked into her brown corduroy skirt, buttons flying; how the bra underneath would be something lacy and colorful, an indication of her true nature. It was all a ruse, he'd discover as that simple motion completely unhinged her and she ran her fingers through his hair and pulled his mouth down to hers, this uptight buttoned-up bit, all part of an elaborate game to drive him crazy, to get him to want what was underneath. In real life, she'd smile at him and raise her coffee mug in an adorably pathetic little salute, and he'd salute back, as he imagined her voice warbling three octaves higher and her hot breath in his ear as he pinned her arms back across the top of the machine and pushed himself into her, making button-shaped imprints in her lower back.

Lately, he felt bad about his fantasies, like the very fact of them constituted adultery. He began to feel overwhelmed by guilt, at nighttime especially, as he lay next to Annie, in those perfect moments just after he'd shut off the light, when anyone looking in on them would think that there was nothing out of the ordinary here, that they were two people lying down for a night of stable, undisturbed sleep. He remembered that this was a sick woman, that he had an extra responsibility to her beyond the obligations he'd come to think of, more or less, as bullshit: holding her on a marital pedestal, pretending that his sexual curiosity shut down the day they began their lives together. This was a person he needed to take care of; she was delicate, and probably frightened. Divorce was one thing, but as long as they were still together, allowing his attention to wander off towards other women was like an act of violence.

His new sense of duty didn't make the fantasies go away. If anything, it made them more urgent, graphic beyond the bounds of anything that had ever roused his interest before, impossible to ignore, and they began to invade his dreams. Once or twice he'd even awoken to the warm stickiness he hadn't felt since he was a teenager, and, like a reflex, the hot flood of shame that went along with it. When he lay down, he'd turn away from her in their bed, squeezing his eyes shut until tears forced their way out, hoping to God that tonight, for once, his thoughts would be pure, or, even better, that he wouldn't dream at all.

11

Halloween was coming, and Miss Ackley told the class to write about what scared them. Thomas liked Miss Ackley a lot. She was young and had short, shiny black hair, as short as a boy's, and sometimes she wore sneakers, which most teachers never did. She had a tattoo of a flower on her wrist. You could see it when she rolled up her sleeves, which she did whenever she got serious. That's how she'd gotten when she gave them this assignment.

"This may be hard for some of you," she'd said. Her voice was a little rough, like someone who had a cold, but it was nice to listen to. "When I say scared, I could mean something like ghosts, or monsters, right? That's what Halloween's all about. Or I could mean something more serious." She looked around at everyone, like she was making sure they were all paying attention. But she didn't really have to; when she got serious, everyone knew it, and everyone listened. "Something happened last year that was very scary. It scared everyone—I promise you, no matter who you talk to, when they saw those airplanes on TV, they were scared. I know I was. And since we live close to where it happened, the fear we felt was even closer, even more real."

Thomas thought about what his mom had said, about her nightmares. Hearing another adult talk about it made him think that his mom must have been telling the truth. He knew his mom didn't lie, but when she said that, it had come out of nowhere. He thought maybe she'd just been treating him like a baby, trying to make him feel better. But now Miss Ackley was saying that she had been scared, too—well, she hadn't said anything about nightmares, but it was good enough for him.

"I promise you that I'll be the only person who reads these," Miss Ackley went on, "so you can write about whatever kind of fear you want."

Then she sat at her desk and read a book and left them to write. She did that a lot; in the beginning kids had moved around and made noise, because even though she was right there, it kind of felt like she'd left them alone in the room. But after a while, everyone started to just put their heads down and write, or at least think. Everyone liked Miss Ackley, Thomas was pretty sure. She reminded him of Ingrid, for some reason. They didn't look anything like each other—Ingrid's hair was light and sort of fluffy, and he couldn't imagine her cutting it off so that it was boy-length—but sometimes he saw her looking at her own wrist when Miss Ackley rolled up her sleeves, and he knew she was thinking about what she would get tattooed there if she could.

Thomas sat in the middle of the room, between Danny Krumm and Allison Nolasco. Danny was fat and chewed the backs of his pens. He put his head really close to the desk when he wrote and stuck his tongue out of the corner of his mouth. Allison was pretty and mean. She had long, reddish hair that covered half of her face while she wrote, like a curtain. Sometimes when he was bored, Thomas imagined pulling her hair back with one hand, so that he could see half of her face, and winking at her. He didn't know why he thought that was so funny.

I'm afraid of bad dreams, he wrote. He was trying to decide whether to describe the airplane dream, or whether Miss Ackley would think that was stupid. Everyone had bad dreams, right? *I know everyone has bad dreams*, he wrote, *and maybe mine aren't worse than anyone else's but sometimes my dreams are so scary they seem real*. He read over what he'd just written. Well, duh, he thought. Of course dreams seemed real—that was the point of dreams, wasn't it? But he kept going. He knew if he stopped to erase every bad idea, he'd never write anything. *My really, really bad dreams make me feel cold after I wake up. They feel like someone hit me. I can't talk in my dreams and I can't move. I always remember my dreams.* He stopped. That was a lie. His mom seemed like she really wanted to know about his dreams, and he'd felt bad that he couldn't tell her. *Some of my dreams are so bad I don't remember them*, he wrote.

Thomas looked around. Everyone else was still writing. He could see Ingrid's back bent over her desk, and her hair falling down to one side. He imagined her perfect, tiny handwriting. He wondered what she was writing about; he couldn't imagine Ingrid being afraid of anything. Maybe she was just making stuff up.

He'd hardly written anything, but he didn't have anything else to say about bad dreams. He wanted to hand in something good to Miss Ackley. He couldn't just write about the airplanes and the towers—everyone was probably writing about that. He tried to think of the scariest thing that had ever happened to him, outside of a dream. It was probably that summer, when he went out to the car to talk to his dad. But that was such a long, boring story, and what was it that he had been scared of, really? If he wrote that, Miss Ackley might just think he was afraid of everything. But he wanted to be honest. Thomas knew that was really important.

One time my parents had a really big fight, Thomas wrote. *It was scary. We were in France. I guess I thought my dad was going to leave.* Thomas read over what he'd written. It didn't really make any sense. But at least he'd been honest. And there was a little more on his paper. But shouldn't there be something else, something that really answered the question?

He thought of writing about his parents changing into monsters. That was something he'd known about for so long that he didn't even really think of it as scary anymore. But even now, as he wrote, he was sure that the three rows of kids behind him had turned into monsters, or disappeared, and that as soon as he turned around to check on them, they'd come back, and up at her desk, Miss Ackley would change. She'd be a big monster, Thomas decided, a fat towering cyclops made of blubber. And she'd have tentacles; he was pretty sure of it.

Thomas started a new line. *I'm also afraid of monsters,* he wrote, and put his pencil down.

When they came back from lunch, Miss Ackley had arranged their desks into their Science Groups. He sat with Ryan Connelly, Brittany

Yee, Alexa Rossi, and Tyler Eakin. He never saw Brittany and Alexa sitting together at lunch or playing together outside, but during their Science Group they acted like best friends. He didn't really like either of them, and he didn't think Ryan did either. He wasn't sure how Tyler felt about anybody; he just talked loudly and got in trouble all the time. Thomas usually ended up kind of reminding everyone about the work they were supposed to be doing. He didn't like that. Sometimes Ryan helped, but Thomas could tell he hated doing that even more than he did; Ryan wasn't very good in school, so it always seemed a little weird for him to be telling other kids who got better grades than him what to do.

Today was tough because they weren't even doing something fun. They were just measuring stuff. Alexa immediately demanded that she should be the person to write the report for the group, and pulled out her sparkly colorful gel pens. Thomas had seen Miss Ackley tell her not to use those pens for assignments before. He decided not to say anything.

"What did you guys write about?" Tyler asked them as soon as Miss Ackley had finished going over the instructions and they were supposed to get to work. "Like for what's scary?" He was dropping the plastic ruler on the floor, picking it up and dropping it again, over and over. No one said anything for a second, so Tyler kept talking. "I wrote about this movie my brother let me watch with him one time, where these guys were vampires and they kept tricking people who wouldn't know they were vampires and then they would bite them on their neck and make *them* vampires too, but like, they had to be in hiding, because people would try to kill the vampires, which is really hard to do, because, like, the vampires will usually bite you first and just make you a vampire."

Ryan was the only one of them who seemed even a little bit interested. "So," he asked Tyler, "it was scary? The movie?"

"Mm-mm." Tyler shook his head. He was still playing with the ruler. "It was really cool, mostly."

"Then why'd you write about it?" said Alexa. She looked up from the sheet of paper where she was still working on writing everyone's name in big, colored-in bubble letters. "You were supposed to write about something *scary*."

"Vampires *are* scary, duh."

"You just said you weren't scared."

"It sounds scary," said Ryan. "I bet I would have been scared. Maybe, like, that's what Miss Ackley meant."

"No," said Brittany. Alexa was sharing her pens with her and she was drawing on the cover of her notebook. "You were supposed to write about something that actually scared you, Miss Ackley totally said that. I wrote about this movie I saw but by accident, that my parents were watching, where this guy had a really scary face with no eyes and a scary deep voice, and then—"

"*You* wrote about a movie too!" said Tyler. "See?"

"No, but listen!" Brittany put down her pen. She moved her hands around when she talked. Thomas thought she might not make a bad teacher when she grew up. "I saw this movie, just a little, little bit of it, and *then* it gave me bad dreams. For like a *week*. Like really bad, scary dreams. So it really *was* scary."

Thomas wondered if he should say something, since he'd written about bad dreams, too, kind of. He didn't know what to say.

"I wrote about spiders," said Ryan. Then he shrugged and didn't say anything else about it.

"You were supposed to write about like a *real* thing," said Alexa. "Like I wrote about when my aunt was sick and going to see her in the hospital. Something like that."

"Spiders are real!" said Ryan. He looked more upset than Thomas had ever seen him.

"Yeah, and uh, I didn't have an aunt that got sick," said Tyler, "so…" He let the ruler hit the floor with a loud *whack*.

Thomas wasn't sure if someone was going to say something like, *What about you, Thomas?* Brittany glanced up at him from drawing for a second but didn't say anything. He looked over at Ingrid's group. It was all girls. She was saying something that made the other girls laugh.

"I thought…" Everyone stopped what they were doing to look at

Thomas when he spoke, even Tyler. "I guess I thought we were supposed to write about, you know. The 9/11 stuff."

"She was just using that as an example," said Alexa.

"Is that what you wrote about?" Ryan asked. Everyone was still looking at him.

He had been more confused than scared when he watched the crash and the people crying and all the other news on TV with his parents that day. The scary part had come later, after they'd been sitting in the living room and watching TV for hours, longer than he was ever usually allowed to, and it was time to go to bed. His dad had turned off the TV and Thomas had gone upstairs to brush his teeth and put on his pajamas—he remembered thinking he wanted one of his parents to come with him, but he knew that was stupid because they hadn't done that since he was really little. Then, when he was in bed, they both came in to say goodnight together, which they didn't usually do.

Thomas remembered being sure that they were going to say something about it, the bad stuff, but then they didn't. Not really. They didn't say that they'd figured out what had happened, and why—wasn't that the point of watching the news, to figure out why stuff was happening? Especially of watching *all day*? They'd just hugged Thomas and kissed him and told him that they loved him. They said it a couple times.

They didn't tell him that everything was going to be OK. Thomas felt dumb for thinking they were going to say that.

Thomas still hadn't answered Ryan's question. Tyler started talking again instead. "My brother saw the planes hit the towers from his window," he said.

Brittany and Alexa looked at each other and rolled their eyes and went back to drawing.

"He did! He saw bodies flying out of the buildings, too."

"He did *not*," said Alexa. "That's impossible."

"Uh, you don't know where he was, so how could you know what he saw?"

"I know he didn't see *that*."

"Hey guys," Thomas said. "Miss Ackley's gonna come over

soon so we should start measuring stuff." He didn't really look at anyone as he talked, and it seemed like no one really heard him.

12

"Do you want me to take the kids trick-or-treating?" Annie asked Paul. She was testing him.

In earlier years, the two of them would go along with a group of other parents, and at the end of the evening they'd all get pizza at Gino's. Annie knew she was whitewashing over some of the less pleasant parts of the evening—itchy costumes, candy complaints, the brief but forceful fights that erupted between the kids—but during that cushy landing at Gino's she always felt like a good parent. Like they were both good parents. The kids would sit at their own table and count candy while she and Paul and whoever the others were—these were kids that Thomas quickly fell out of friendship with, since these days he didn't really express interest in anyone his age except Ingrid—would discuss something boring and benign. They were young parents, and their lives were filled with soft, safe things.

"Sure!" His answer was quick, and insulting. Not only had he not acknowledged that this was a change from the norm, or offered to help; he clearly hadn't spent even a second feeling nostalgic. *He thinks he's too good for nostalgia*, she thought. *Or just can't feel it. Fucking robot.*

"I could use a night to myself," he added, and he may have said thanks then but she was disgusted and left the room.

He might have also been punishing her for not finding a doctor yet. He hadn't brought it up in about a week, and she knew it was a long shot, but she'd hoped he'd just forgotten about it.

But that night, in a silence before dinner, when their paths crossed in the kitchen, he'd asked her how the search was coming, and she'd told him that she'd been swamped at work and that she'd look tomorrow.

That Friday, Ingrid came over with Thomas after school, carrying an oversized paper bag with slivers of glittery fabric peeking over the top. Annie was sure Ingrid's mother, Lydia, had handcrafted some breathtaking costume; she and Thomas had poked around Target for about half an hour until she found the Robin Hood costume, which he shrugged at and said he wouldn't mind wearing. *You get what you put in*, Annie thought, and often thought when she saw Ingrid; Lydia braided tiny flowers into her hair, sewed patches onto her jeans that looked like they came from dresses that Annie couldn't afford. A little kid had no business looking that fashionable; when Annie saw Ingrid, she felt relieved to have a boy, and some excuse not to work out her own style insecurities on him.

Ingrid creeped her out. She and Thomas were almost exactly the same height, and when they stood next to each other they looked ghostly, like a black-and-white photograph of sickly children a hundred years ago. Before Ingrid came over to play for the first time, Annie had never seen another child with the same degree of unwavering seriousness. Since he was her own child, Annie had found various ways to think of Thomas as unusual in a beautiful way; she was blessed with a strange, brilliant boy, she attempted to remind herself when she felt that foreign feeling insert itself between them. Sometimes he still took her by surprise—his too-pale eyes that must have come from some distant branch of Paul's family, the way his mouth naturally turned down—but she tried to imagine how this strangeness would translate itself in ten years: he'd be a brooding painter, or a writer. He'd have that temperament that would make sense in retrospect when people studied his work years later.

But the scary conclusions Annie resisted drawing about Thomas came easily with Ingrid. She was a pale, otherworldly child, impervious to joy or humor, sizing up the world around her with a cold precision that had no business existing in someone so young. She was menacing.

Thomas loved her, of course, which was the worst part. She was a bad influence, silently encouraging him to move towards the adult part of him, away from the child. He was also too young to love someone. She thought he should have other friends, and love them all, with a child's flimsy affection. When Annie told him once that Lydia had called to say that Ingrid was sick and couldn't come over, he'd furrowed his eyebrows with a concern that was supposed to be reserved for adults. Married adults.

"I haven't been to your house in a long time," Ingrid said as Annie held the door open for them.

"That's true," said Thomas. "It's about the same as the last time you were here. A little darker."

"Darker?" Annie repeated, stopping them in their tracks on their way up the stairs. "Did you say darker?"

Thomas dropped his head, as if he had been caught, then shrugged.

"What do you mean, sweetie?"

Thomas shrugged again. "I dunno. It's just darker."

Ingrid was looking right at her, like a disapproving teacher waiting for the last noisy kid to quiet down. "I was just wondering," Annie said dismissively. "Go upstairs and get changed."

Annie thought she should offer the kids a snack so that they wouldn't nosh on their candy as they went along—what would Lydia say if Ingrid came home with a half-empty bag?—but when she found them at the foot of the stairs, their uniform stares were all business; they hadn't come to loiter. Annie pressed her lips together, raised her eyebrows and smiled too wide, the host of a party for people she didn't know. "You guys look great," she said. "Let's go."

It was only a partial lie. Ingrid looked great, although Annie didn't know whether she was supposed to be a fairy or a butterfly or some other little girl fantasy, and she didn't ask, since she tried to avoid talking to her. She'd applied her own makeup, with surprising sophistication, so that in certain lights her cheeks glowed with a quiet sparkle. Lydia had outdone herself with the costume: a white leotard, splashed with an elaborate sparkling paisley pattern in pink and purple, and a pair of wings wider than Ingrid was tall, dripping with lines of some kind of high-end tinsel, thicker and more mature than the kind that ended up all over Annie's floor every Christmas. She was pretty, but not in a sloppy kid's way; she was picturesque, like some slice-of-life photography exhibit: *Ingrid, Age 8, on Halloween.* What was missing was the enthusiasm. Annie didn't know how much Lydia and Greg worked on positive body image stuff with Ingrid, told her she was beautiful and all that, but she knew that, at eight years old, the little girl's indifference to her own appearance was what her twenty-something employees seemed to spend most of their energy trying to cultivate.

Thomas looked like a bored kid in a Robin Hood costume. The feather in his cap drooped over his right eye, his bow dragged on the ground, seconds from slipping out of his fingers, and he fidgeted with the strap of the plastic quiver slung across his shoulder.

"Jackets," she said, and watched as they rolled their eyes and removed their whimsical appendages and covered them in thick earth tones, their fun smothered by practicality. The way they looked at her communicated the sad paradox of Halloween, that they may as well not be wearing costumes if the point was to keep warm. Annie wondered why, somewhere along the line, whoever came up with trick-or-treating hadn't thought to move Halloween to a more costume-appropriate season. Why couldn't that guy be on the receiving end of those stares?

Even though Court and Smith Streets were lined with stores that gave out candy, they'd always start off by going door-to-door on the residential streets, to simulate a real, non-New York Halloween. You'd think Paul was putting it on, the way he talked about his holidays—his whole childhood, really—all pies and ceremony, the Abells next door and the Shepards across the street, the same thing every year, like a slowly evolving Norman Rockwell painting. Annie never knew her neighbors' last names, and she'd never considered that a bad thing either, but hearing about his upbringing made her feel self-conscious, and she could see the value in Thomas having some version of familiarity, even if it was just recognizing the woman they sometimes saw in the bagel store as the person who'd answer the door on Clinton and Union.

She did like Carroll Gardens on nights like this. The sidewalks were dominated by pudgy figures in brown and gray with bright colors poking out, their mittened hands clutching grinning plastic pumpkin-heads, like backstage passes to an exclusive kids' meeting. Taller figures, mostly women, towered behind them, huddling their arms close to their bodies, unsure of how to keep a safe distance. Doors opened and closed periodically, and an old lady would pop out and coo her approval, *how scary, how pretty*—then the thunder of bulk candy in plastic, and then the door would close again.

On Halloween, everyone's children were interchangeable. There was nothing biological, no ethereal whispering of a mother's heart that dictated that a Robin Hood belonged to her any more than a ghost or a ubiquitous Disney animal. Annie wasn't adventurous enough to pick a child and imagine herself into an alternate life, where she was that kid's mother and whatever balding paunchy man trotting along behind him was the man she lay down next to every night. But she was eminently aware, tonight especially, that any of these situations *could* be true.

As the night went on, she allowed a greater distance to stretch out between her and the kids. It was clear that they didn't see the evening as an opportunity to spend quality time with her. Her own mother would have said, "I understand, who wants their mother around any-way? Don't mind me." Instead, she stayed silent, six, then seven, then eight paces behind, watched their backs as they huddled close to one another and moved from stoop to stoop, symmetrical, like paper dolls, like someone had made them that way. They almost seemed to sway.

On Atlantic Avenue, where the streets opened up and the number of cars and children thickened and spilled over into something con-fused and metropolitan, she waited while Ingrid and Thomas knocked on the door of the Tripoli. The owner, a well-groomed older Lebanese man, recognized Thomas by now—he was, according to the old man, the only little boy he'd ever met who liked rose water. She leaned against the building and looked across the four-lane avenue to the unsightly mix of Subways and Duane Reades that lay on the other side.

She almost didn't notice the light pressure against her thigh; some-thing warm was wrapping itself around her, and the feeling was familiar, but one she hadn't felt in a long time. She liked this new warmth, and instinctively reached her hand down to find the source and hold it close to her. Annie's fingers found hair: the cool, smooth head of a small person, their face smushed against her out of a need for safety. For whomever this was, she looked, from a distance, like that safety.

"Connor!"

A woman's voice came from across Clinton Street; she didn't recognize it, but there was no mistaking the shrill urgency of a mother afraid for her young. Annie's fingers splayed out like she had touched something hot. The child she was touching was a stranger.

She was not this little boy's mother. She was just another tall being. He'd gravitated towards her because of her size and because he was stupid, a little animal. Her own child was somewhere else.

The little boy lifted his head and looked up at her. His mouth hung open, but not out of fear or confusion or any of the anchors that held down Thomas's every movement. He was simply a child, overwhelmed by a world of sights and sounds he didn't understand yet, and he'd made a mistake. It made so much sense Annie thought she might cry.

The boy's mother must have run across the street without looking at the light, because Annie swore she was there the second after she'd heard her voice. "Connor!" she said again, snatching the boy away, pulling him away from Annie's body, so quickly that her body had no time to remember the sensation of his warmth. "Do *not* walk ahead without me again, you hear me!"

She didn't say anything to Annie. She didn't even look at her. It was worse than getting yelled at; as far as this woman was concerned, Annie was simply an object standing between her and her son. There was no such thing as a universal language of mothers.

"Mom?"

Thomas and Ingrid were standing in the doorway of the Tripoli, their once-empty pillowcases now sagging on either side of them. Annie wondered how long they'd been standing there, and whether Thomas had seen her touch the head of a strange child who wasn't him.

"We're ready to go."

Annie nodded and gestured for them to lead the way, then followed them east towards Court Street.

What does that even *mean*, she thought, the house has gotten *darker*?

After she left Ingrid with her mother and Thomas ran up to his room, she walked into their living room to find Paul in the most infuriating place he could have been, in front of the TV. She was ready to say something then, really say something. She was running on humiliation and frustration and exhaustion, and there he was, drinking a beer, the blue light painting his face.

"Have you found a doctor yet?"

She imagined what she must look like, damp from the drizzle that started on their walk home, her hair escaping its rubber band on either side, her skin beginning to register the grease from the two pizza slices she'd been too lazy to pat down with a napkin first, her body mocked by the unflattering winter coat that bulked out all around her like a garbage bag. He should have been a lawyer, the fucking sadist, going for it right when she was at her most vulnerable.

She was tired. God, she was so tired.

"Oh," she said, "didn't I tell you?" Paul looked up. "I thought I told you."

He looked pleased. He looked—she hated to admit it—handsome this way, like a man who liked her and was waiting for her to speak.

"I found a name yesterday, and I made an appointment." Annie was sure she was shaking, or smiling too much.

But unless he was planning an elaborate sting operation later, as far as she could tell, he didn't suspect anything. He grinned. "That's great! What's his name? Or her name, I guess? What's the doctor's name?"

"Scheckman," she answered automatically. "Stephen Scheckman." The name, which had been staring up at her from a Post-it note she'd stuck on her desk at work weeks ago, bubbled to the surface of her mind before she even fully remembered that it belonged to an actual sleep disorder specialist in midtown.

Paul's smile softened into something more approving; maybe, subconsciously, he'd suspected that she was bluffing and wanted a piece of hard evidence. Or, just as likely, he was pleased to hear a Jewish name. Paul espoused a casual, backwards anti-Semitism that believed the only worthwhile doctors and lawyers were Jews.

Normally, she would have called him on this; at a different time, they might have even joked about it. But she needed to keep her composure now, to get away from the lie in one piece.

"Yup," she continued, "I'm going to see him on Monday and Wednesday. And, I guess, if I like him, Mondays and Wednesdays after that."

Paul was looking at her as if she'd just revealed a talent he'd never known about before. He was looking at her the way men look at women in movies, just before the ending, when she's done something really extraordinary and he remembers why he fell in love with her in the first place. Annie knew she was getting carried away; he was just excited that, finally, he wouldn't have to worry about her getting up and wandering away in the middle of the night. Still, the look meant something. She felt warm, remembering older versions of him, when she used to see it more often.

"I'm tired," she said, without planning to. Like the name from the Post-it, it rose to the surface, because it was a truth.

Paul nodded. "Well, get some sleep then," he said. "I'll be up in a bit." Another exchange that could have passed for normal; someone looking in would have no idea, would they, that anything was wrong here. Maybe, Annie thought, smiling in spite of herself, nothing *was* wrong, at the moment.

"Hey," he said, waving the remote in her direction without looking away from the TV. "Thanks for taking the kids tonight." He turned the volume down on the car commercial screaming at them in the background, then added, again, "I really did need a night to myself."

She didn't respond. He'd left her with that creepy kid, and she'd petted a strange child's head like a predator, and their son thought the house was darker. Where was everyone getting the idea that she was supposed to understand these imaginary implications? Halloween is a *tradition*, she wanted to say, for us, for all of us. Don't you remember?

But instead she nodded, and went to bed, and the next day she went into work intending to throw the Post-it away, but instead she stuck it to the bottom of the desk drawer she never used.

She sat with Thomas until he fell asleep. "Did you see any scary costumes?" she asked.

"Um," he said. With his eyes closed, he could have been any age. He could have been a baby. "I saw a man dressed as that guy—what's his name, the one who sent the planes to the buildings?"

Annie sighed. She'd seen him, too. More than one, actually. She'd thought of saying something, walking up to some nineteen-year-old kid and telling him that there were children in this neighborhood, children who were too young to understand their hip backwards sense of humor, that maybe they should save their tasteless attempts at cultural commentary for a party with their idiot friends—but she'd already made a fool of herself once that evening, so she'd just hoped Thomas hadn't noticed.

"His name is Osama bin Laden," she said. "Did that scare you?"

Thomas sat up. He shrugged. "I guess not," he said. "He just looked like a man." He looked at her for a moment; maybe her expression was giving him something other than what a mother was supposed to give, endless support and love. Maybe she looked disappointed, or even bored. She didn't know how to fix that.

"I didn't see any real monsters," he said brightly, as if she had asked him for some good news. "That would have been scary."

Annie nodded. Thomas lay back down and she stroked his hair until she felt his breathing steady into sleep. Maybe she should have taken the opportunity to teach him, as Paul would have—explained why, when you get older, you become less afraid of monsters and more afraid of people.

13

Where's Dad?

In the middle of the night, Thomas had woken up. He didn't know how long he'd been asleep. The French night seemed about the same as the American night. Quieter. Darker, maybe.

Usually when he woke up in a strange place, he was confused for a while, but for some reason, he knew exactly where he was: he was in France, in a town just south of Paris, according to his dad—he'd forgotten the name, but he was pretty sure it started with a B—in a cottage surrounded by other cottages, under a scratchy gray blanket. And his dad still wasn't there. He couldn't hear or see anything in the dark, but he knew that part. He was sure of it.

He thought of the inside-outside game that he'd play with himself late at night at home: if I just got out of bed, if I just walked outside, if I just walked to the subway. Everything was still there, except this time it was a different set of everything—the places his father had shown him in the Michelin books: Germany. England. Spain. All he had to do was put his feet on the floor.

Thomas sat up, which usually felt scary enough to make him lie back down right away. It was a little cold, but less scary than usual. Maybe even not at all. He moved the covers away and stood up. It was late at night, and he was out of bed.

He stood very still and tried not to breathe, so he could hear if his mom was awake. After listening to a few long breaths in and out, he realized he didn't really know what his mother sounded like when she slept. He liked the sound he heard, even if it was just a monster doing an imitation.

He had been right: it was just that easy. He was at the front door. No one stopped him as he pushed down the hundred-year-old door handle—everything in Europe was old, his dad had said—and when he walked outside, no one told him to come back.

He'd never been anywhere as quiet as the courtyard at night. In the morning, there were people around, plates clinking, sometimes even a couple of chickens wandering around and clucking to themselves like they didn't care about anything. Now, no one was here, and there was no noise, not even a cricket. The stars seemed brighter here, because the sky was so dark. It was like someone had taken a sheet of black construction paper and ripped little holes in it, just to mess something up.

It wasn't too cold and he wasn't tired. There were no monsters near here, no planes flying into buildings, no mother and no father. There was nothing except him, and he could go anywhere. For a second, the dark didn't seem as dark.

Where would he go?

Then he heard something: gravel crunching, slow and quiet, getting louder.

A light spread across the path in front of him, which led out to the big road and the town that started with a B. He saw the sunflower field on the other side of the road—it was clear for a moment, like a black-and-white photo, then it disappeared. Then the light shone right on him, and it was much brighter this time, almost blinding.

He'd heard about something like this before, something about a bright light, but he couldn't remember where. For some reason, he thought of his mom, asleep. Really, he was only a few feet away from the cottage. He could run back there, if only he could move.

Then the light shut off, and the world wobbled in and out until the bright spinning spots faded and he was in the dark again.

The car was close enough that he could reach out and touch the hood. His dad was there, looking out; Thomas couldn't tell if he was looking at him or not.

"Dad?"

It felt like no one had said anything for hundreds of years.

His dad didn't say anything when Thomas opened the car door and sat down next to him. He still had his hands on the wheel. He didn't even look up.

"Dad?" he said again. "Are you OK?"

His dad breathed in and out a few times before he said anything. "No, Thomas. Not really."

Thomas was glad to hear his dad say his name.

"Where did you go?"

His dad didn't say anything.

Thomas wondered if maybe he hadn't heard him. He was pretty sure he had.

"Are you gonna come back inside?"

He still didn't say anything; this time, he closed his eyes. Sometimes he did that to help him think better, but sometimes he just did it when he thought Thomas was being annoying. Thomas didn't know which one this was. After a while, his dad said, "I don't know."

That didn't make sense. Thomas had thought he was going to say, "In a minute." He was sure of it.

Thomas didn't say anything then. He thought maybe it was his dad's turn to say something, like ask him what he was doing outside in the middle of the night or if it had been scary when the car came so close to him. It hadn't really—it was more surprising than any-thing—but he wanted him to ask anyway.

His dad kept not saying anything, kept staring straight ahead. Thomas looked where he was looking; there was nothing there but the lit-up side of their little cottage. He thought of his mom in there, a monster in the quiet, waiting to attack the first person that walked through the door.

"Dad?" Finally, his father turned his head towards him, but slowly, as if he couldn't quite remember what Thomas was doing there. "What's gonna happen now?"

His dad said, "I don't know."

That was not what Thomas was expecting him to say at all. It was a big, difficult question, and his dad always had answers for those. Long, smart answers. He never just didn't *know*.

"Are you going to leave?"

He didn't know exactly what that meant until after he'd said it. He meant was his dad going to leave and make him and his mom go back to Brooklyn by themselves. He never would have imagined that he'd think something like that could happen, but tonight it made a lot of sense, and he wanted to know, and he thought he might go crazy if his father said "I don't know" again.

"Thomas, I'm in the middle of France. I can't leave while we're here, I don't know where I am."

That almost sounded like a joke. He wished his dad had looked at him once while he said it, so that he could know that he'd meant it that way.

Thomas knew he should go back inside. But there was one more thing he had to ask. When he spoke, his voice was the tiniest noise in France.

"Are you going to leave when we get home?"

His father waited a long time to answer. He wished he knew whether he was thinking about the answer, or about something else.

"I don't know."

Thomas started to cry. Then he got out of the car, ran back inside and got into bed. He realized he'd been wearing his pajamas this whole time. Had he really planned to walk to Spain in his pajamas?

He didn't fall sleep. He didn't know how long he lay there before he heard the door open and close and saw his dad's long, skinny shadow move along to the wall until it stopped at the bed and faded away.

That was a bad time, but things were better now. He was excited to tell Ingrid that part; he still hadn't told her the whole France story, but he was beginning to think he didn't have to, because pretty soon everything would be back to normal.

Their side of the playground was quiet, except Ingrid's creaking as she swung back and forth. It was too cold to be on the swings, really, which everyone except Ingrid seemed to understand. Thomas leaned against the leg of the swing set, blowing in his hands the way he'd seen adults do. Every couple of seconds, Ingrid's pink tights and dirty white sneaker would fly by the side of his face.

"Are your parents getting along?" she asked. "Did they stop fighting?"

He had to think about that. "They're not fighting," he said, after a minute. Had they ever really fought, the way she meant it? Loudly, with yelling and all that? Even in France, there had just been a lot of fast, angry talking. When Ingrid talked about her parents in the last months before the divorce, she made it sound like they tore the house down with their screaming. Thomas's parents never did anything like that. They just frowned at each other a lot, and got really quiet when he walked out of the room like they were waiting to talk about something important.

Of course, they could have just been waiting to turn into monsters. Thomas hadn't told Ingrid about that. He knew he could still tell her anything, but lately there were more and more little secrets like that, things he just wasn't sure about.

"So it's better?" she asked. Thomas noticed that she swung back and forth exactly the same distance every time, and that the swing was singing a little song that never changed. Only Ingrid could make swings work like that.

"Well," he said, "sort of. My mom's not around on Monday and Wednesday nights. She doesn't get home until after I go to bed." Ingrid didn't say anything. Thomas wondered if she knew something, if there was some divorced kid secret he was missing. "And my dad's being a lot nicer to her. I mean kind of." He thought for a second. "She's about the same, I guess. I don't know."

"Where does she go?"

"What?"

Ingrid stuck her legs out straight in front of her, and the swing slowed and sort of floated her down. When she stopped, her feet didn't scuff around in the dirt the way his did. They just rested. Thomas looked out at the rest of the playground. Kids were clumped together in different parts, not really playing with anything. What were they doing, he wondered, when they just stood around like that? What was he missing?

"Where does your mom go," she asked, "on Monday and Wednesday nights?"

"A doctor," he said. "Some kind of doctor, my dad told me."

Ingrid didn't say anything for a while. Thomas knew she was probably thinking something smart about what it all meant. He knew that Ingrid was smarter than him, but he didn't like to ask her to tell him the things she knew. He liked it when she chose to tell him, on her own, like when his dad gave him Awesome Lessons; that was when he felt special.

"Well," she said, "it sounds to me like things are a lot better."

The bell rang. All the other kids ran into the door of the gym, their mittens flapping out from the ends of their arms like tentacles.

14

Annie thought she was the last one in the store when she left on Wednesday evening, but before she could turn out the master lights she ran into Dana, balancing her Closing checklist clipboard in the crook of her arm and examining a cookbook.

"Good night," Annie called to her, and Dana looked up, startled.

"Oh. G'night, Annie. Sorry, I thought I was the only one here. I'll lock up."

Annie could see a hint of something hot and yellowy in a white dish on the open page in Dana's arm. Even from here, it looked too complicated for anyone to ever attempt. Dana was twenty-two or twenty-three; she wore baggy cardigans and tight black jeans and thick-framed glasses that may or may not have had real lenses in them. Annie couldn't imagine her cooking.

She stayed for a second, and thought of the things people might say to each other in a moment like this: she could ask about the cookbook, or say something like, "Got any big plans for the evening?" She felt embarrassed even thinking about saying that.

Why wouldn't she cook? she wondered, as she walked by Dana, waving wordlessly. *She could be a master chef. She could be anything. I don't know anything about her at all.*

She decided to walk to the river. The river—as a city kid, she'd always liked the sound of that, and had stubbornly kept it far away in her mind, even if that wasn't always the truth. She still imagined it from the poster that had hung in her fifth-grade classroom, brilliant blue and curving playfully between the lumpy green Catskills. *The Mighty Hudson!* the poster proclaimed, in an attempt to remind students that they were part of something bigger, outside of New York City. Sometimes it was still hard to believe.

It was 6:30. She didn't have to be home for another three, three and a half hours. Her evening was wide open. That hadn't been true in years. The week before, she'd seen a movie at a multiplex, then snuck into another one, which she hadn't done since she was a kid. Before that, she'd gone to a gay bar on 8th Avenue, which made her think of Eddie, her old roommate and childhood friend. She hadn't spoken to him in years, probably since before Thomas was born; she should give him a call, she thought, and wondered, *Would that even have occurred to me if I hadn't come here? When would I ever have the time to remember people and places from former lives, if all I ever did was work and go home, if the only people I ever saw were my husband and my kid?*

This was the kind of wandering she appreciated, the kind of wandering fully-grown people were supposed to do. She was in charge of her body, and not the other way around. These fake doctor days were the magical thing she'd been waiting for: evenings to rediscover old places and find new ones, all on her own, all with no one else to answer to. She felt like a teenager again, and she'd never been happier than when she was a teenager, when she and her friends were invincible young New Yorkers, who knew that they were ahead of everyone else in the country, that they could go anywhere and be the savviest kids in the room.

At home, Paul seemed happier. When the three of them were together, he invited her to share in his Awesome Lessons, which he'd never done before. Annie had to admit she could see why they'd be appealing to an eight-year-old boy. Inspired by a conversation with his dad one night when she wasn't there, Thomas had developed a voracious academic interest in Elvis Presley. Paul dug up some of his old records, printed out color pictures of Graceland, and even found *Kissin' Cousins* and *Fun in Acapulco* at the video store, to sample the King's acting career. They weren't sure Thomas appreciated how hysterically awful they were, but he laughed at the jokes Paul made as they watched, and Annie remembered how that used to be their favorite thing to do, watch terrible movies and talk so much that whoever they were watching with would get annoyed and leave.

Her only lingering disquiet came from having to be away from Thomas for two full days each week. She was aware that he was at an age when life moved quickly; she didn't want to be one of those mothers who turned around and suddenly found her son was a teenager, unwilling to even be seen with her in public. Thomas was moving even faster along that path than most children, since he was part adult already. This was a golden age in their relationship; her fear of him was slowly being replaced by a genuine appreciation, a respect most people would reserve for someone their own age. He had something strange and beautiful to offer her, and there were things she wanted to share with him, too; things Paul couldn't give him.

She covered her tracks. She meticulously imagined each visit with Dr. Stephen Scheckman. It was almost fun, and, she reasoned, almost like designing a therapeutic regimen for herself, if only second-hand.

Dr. Scheckman was thorough, but not pushy. He asked her about her childhood, and wrote as she spoke, his calm, unchanging expression an inscrutable wall. He never betrayed so much as a sniff to indicate judgment. He was good.

"Good!" Paul said as she reported back to him after her first visit, sitting in his chair and watching her as if she were giving a recital. "Annie, this is really good news."

Well, he shouldn't celebrate just yet, she told him; according to Scheckman, it might take quite a while before they would see any real change. Sleepwalking was a deep-rooted disorder, and dismantling it required hard work and a fair bit of psychological digging around.

"I understand," he said, but she thought she detected something—disappointment? nervousness?—behind his supportive frown. "You're getting help, and that's what's important. I'm really proud of you," he said, placing his hand on hers.

In the meantime, Scheckman encouraged locking the bedroom window while they slept, and not a whole lot else. *Why not?* she thought. Part of her also knew, reluctantly, that it wasn't such a bad idea for other reasons.

Scheckman had her keep a journal. Annie was particularly proud of this invention; she thought it added a layer of realism. She made a big deal of showing Paul the lovely leather-bound journal she'd picked out for herself with her employee discount, and kept it in the drawer in her nightstand. She'd wait until it was completely silent before she opened the drawer and clicked her pen, so that he'd know that she was, at that moment, the most responsible person in the room.

Then she just kept a journal. That's all Scheckman had asked of her, after all. He didn't even care if she talked about sleep-walking, specifically. He just wanted her to have a record of her feelings and behavior, so that they could really get to the bottom of things. She recorded her feelings and her behavior. There was no point in not being honest.

Maybe it was her imagination, but it felt to Annie as if the sleep-walking did slow down, ever so slightly. Often she'd wake up in the middle of the night, and panic, for a moment, as if she was in a strange place. But then she'd discover that everything around her was smooth and warm, and that gravity was anchoring her, almost pulling her in. She'd stretch her arms out into a snow angel, wanting to feel the soft safety of the sheets. If her pinky brushed Paul's side, he'd murmur something in sleep-language that sounded happy, or at least content.

It was OK, Annie thought as she waited for the light to change at the West Side Highway. She wasn't, as she had orig-inally thought, killing time until she decided to call the real Stephen Scheckman; the imagined Scheckman was doing a fine job already. And what if he wanted to schedule a different night? She'd come to depend on Wednesdays. She couldn't remember how she'd gotten through the week without them.

I looked at Hoboken tonight, she wrote, after she'd come home and kissed Thomas good night, while Paul slept beside her, subconsciously registering the scratching next to him and silently approving, agree-ing. *One of the most boring places I've ever had the misfortune to visit, but across the Hudson, it's magnificent. I stood there forever. Didn't even notice when it started to get unbearably cold. I never thought of myself as someone who could spend her time just looking like that, but there I was. Perhaps I will go more often.*

She liked capping her evenings off like this. Maybe it was what made sleep so much more restful lately. Maybe this was the cure.

15

Thomas liked to play with Alexander, but there's only so much a turtle can do, so playing usually just meant hide-and-seek. Alexander would go inside his house, the curved rock with the opening cut out of it, and get pretty far back in there so that it was too dark to see him. Then Thomas would pretend to look all over the room for him, and finally he'd come back to the tank and sigh and go, "I give up, I have no idea where he could be," and he'd tap on the glass and then Alexander would poke his head out, looking satisfied.

Ingrid had showed him how she could get Fraidy to jump really high in the air by waving a feather thing around in front of her, and then Fraidy would go crazy trying to get it. Alexander wasn't a jumper. He liked walking around and eating. Thomas wasn't sure he even liked hiding, but he'd play hide-and-seek anyway. Maybe he knew Thomas was bored. That was nice of him, he thought.

Sometimes it surprised him that he and Alexander got along so well, considering that Alexander was, technically, a monster. Any animal without fur was a monster; some with fur were monsters too, if they had long enough claws or sharp enough teeth. He'd even surprised himself when he asked for a turtle in the first place; but when his dad had asked him if he wanted a hamster or something instead, he had been sure.

He liked Alexander when he could see him, at least. Sometimes, at night, he'd start to think about him in his log house and he'd forget what he looked like; his brain would make him bigger, with small, slitted eyes, like a snake. Sometimes, if Thomas turned his head quickly to look at the tank in the dark, he thought he could see little red spots peering out at him. Sometimes they were yellow. But then they'd go away.

He'd been playing for a while when his dad came in. He stood in the doorframe and knocked on the door from the inside. Thomas hated when adults did that; it was completely unnecessary, and they obviously just thought they were being cute.

"Hey, old pal," his dad said. "Wanna do something?"

Thomas looked at the tank. He was already doing something, he wanted to say, but didn't. "Are you bored too, Dad?"

"Bored?" his dad came in and sat on the bed. "Why would you say that? We've just got some time before you have to go to bed and I thought maybe you'd like to hang out." Thomas didn't say anything, and his dad looked around at stuff like he was trying to find something—the bedspread, the window, his watch. "Did you finish all your homework?" he said finally.

Thomas nodded, and thought, *Shouldn't he have asked about that first?* Maybe his dad really was bored. Or maybe he'd been a monster too long that night, and forgot how to be a human dad.

"OK," his dad said, "so let's play cards or something."

Thomas didn't know if they had any cards in their house. He and his dad had never played cards together. Sometimes, all three of them played I Spy in the car. That was about it for games. His parents knew that he was happy to sit on the carpet and play with trucks or Legos by himself. Besides, now he had Alexander, which was like having a whole new person to play with.

He tried to think of something he did want to do with his dad, something that would actually be fun. "Can I have an Awesome Lesson?" he asked.

His dad nodded slowly, as if that was a brilliant idea he never would have thought of himself. "An Awesome Lesson, hmm? I suppose we could do that." He looked back towards the hallway, then back at Thomas. "I'm not sure how much more I know about Elvis though, old pal, to be completely honest."

"That's OK," said Thomas. "We can be done with Elvis now."

"Music to my ears," his dad said. "OK, sit tight for a minute and let me prepare a few things."

Thomas sat on the edge of the bed and waited while his dad went across the hall to his study. Alexander was hiding again—he didn't know that they were done playing, for now. Soon he'd figure it out, though, when Thomas didn't look around the room for him. Then he'd just go to sleep. Or whatever it was he did in there. Maybe Alexander changed, too; Thomas had never thought of that before. Why not? Maybe when he couldn't see him, his turtle became a human.

His dad came back with a photo album and a map. Thomas had seen the photo album before. "OK." He sat down next to him on the bed and opened the album. "Now, this place—you know this place, right?"

Thomas nodded and said that it was Grandma and Grandpa's house in New Hampshire, where they were going for Thanksgiving.

"Right," his dad said. "So since we're going to be in Tuftonboro soon, I figured we should have a couple Awesome Lessons about it first. A well-informed traveler always researches their destination beforehand." Thomas nodded. He couldn't argue with that. He remembered the Awesome Lessons about France; they'd watched a movie about a boy who chased a magical red balloon around Paris, and he and his mom made little pancakes and spread chocolate on them. They didn't taste great, but he didn't care; he thought it was really cool that she'd already known what they would eat before they even got there.

"Tuftonboro," his dad said, pointing to the map, "is on Lake Winnipesaukee. That's an Indian name; it means 'impossible to pronounce.'"

Thomas smiled. He did like Awesome Lessons. His dad did, too; he could tell. Thomas didn't know anything about chemistry, but he'd always secretly hoped that someday he'd be able to be in his dad's class. He bet his dad was a pretty good chemistry professor.

They spent the rest of the evening on the Awesome Lesson. His dad told him about the white signs that were the same outside the library and the post office and the town hall, and the elementary school playground where he learned to ride a bike. He showed Thomas on the map how technically he grew up on the outskirts of central Tuftonboro, in the southwestern corner, so they were right on the lake. He and his younger brother Joe both knew how to swim by the time they were four. Thomas asked him if that meant without swimmies or a kickboard.

"We didn't use kickboards back then," his dad said, "and swimmies are for sissies." Then he laughed. Thomas thought the joke was corny but he laughed too. He laughed anyway, because he felt good.

Annie stood outside a bar on 37th Street, west of 8th Avenue. It was called Murphy's, or O'Leary's, or some other ubiquitous Irish name—they all looked the same to her: deep green awning, jolly font, fading gold embellishments. The sign hanging above the door showed a cartoon toucan with a beer perched on its beak. "Lovely Day for a Guinness," it said. The lack of imagination at these places irritated her; the sign was supposed to be quirky, but every place on this block had one exactly like it. They weren't even trying.

The inside was also unsurprising: big and dark. Three boulder-shaped men sat at the bar, two together in the middle, and a guy in a denim jacket on the end, by himself. It was Wednesday night, and most people were elsewhere. That was her place in the social order: the husband and kid waiting for her in the apartment in Brooklyn were supposed to be a gift, God's way of saying that she was allowed to not spend her evenings in places like this, ever, if she didn't want to.

There were several booths along the windowless right wall, which seemed the logical place for her to shrink away, maybe eat something, maybe squint over a book in the dim light. There had probably been other people like her in here at some point, who were killing time before a play or needed a place to duck out of the rain or heat or cold. But somehow that seemed to defeat the purpose. And there was a purpose—if nothing else, these evenings had to have that; otherwise she was just a liar avoiding her family.

She surveyed the bar. If she sat between the two men who were together and the guy in the denim jacket, she'd be vulnerable, floating in the middle of the ocean. She had to anchor herself next to someone. She chose the man in the denim jacket, since he was alone.

Annie had to worm her way up onto the bar stool, a position she wasn't used to. The man in the denim jacket left her no room—he might not have even noticed her appear next to him; he was so huge he was probably shielded from outside stimuli by the protective bubble of his size. Her ascent ended clumsily, and she toppled into him a little. She didn't have time to compose an expression that would make it clear that the maneuver hadn't been intentional before he turned to look at her.

The man's face didn't just clash with his body; it clashed with his entire setting. He had long eyelashes, a sweet little punctuation mark of a nose and a diminutive mouth that Annie imagined he could make disappear if he moved his lips the right way. His eyes were an inky dark brown, soft and thoughtful. Nothing about him was rough except his stubble, which was even and inviting; it looked like he maintained it.

He nodded at her. "Annie," she said, and that was it: she'd decided, for both of them, that they were going to stop being strangers.

"I'm Jack," he said.

"I like that name," she said, which was true. If she just kept saying things that were more or less true, she thought, she should be more or less OK.

Jack nodded again. "Are you drinking, Annie?"

Her stomach untied in a way she hadn't felt in a long time. Something about hearing him say her name felt promising, and thinking in terms of promise made her feel wobbly on the barstool.

"Yes," she said. "I'd like—" It hadn't occurred to her until now how infrequently she drank. She didn't think about it, because she didn't really miss it. She had drunk, occasionally, in college—but what was it she used to like? "Do they have cider here?" she asked, then felt stupid for asking him instead of the bartender.

Jack laughed, but without malice. "Yup. Hold on. Hey, Sean—"

The bartender was young, a skinny redhead with his sleeves rolled up. He spread his arms out on the bar and leaned towards them. "What can I get you," he said, looking back and forth between the two of them.

"She'll have a Magner's," Jack said, "and another scotch and soda for me, please."

The bartender said sure thing and disappeared to the other end of the bar. Annie rubbed her sweaty palms on her pant legs, unsure of what was supposed to happen next.

Jack asked her what she did. She thought it seemed like such a pro-saic dinner party question for the setting... But then again, what was so exotic about a bar, to people who weren't her?

"I work at a restaurant on the Upper West Side." The lie tingled in her groin.

Jack nodded again and didn't ask for any more specifics. Annie wondered if he knew she was making it up, if that was a given in interactions like this. She wondered how much of what he'd say to her would be lies.

"What brings you down here, then?" he asked. "Night off?"

Instinctively she feared that he was trying to catch her, before she remembered that, unlike her husband, this stranger had no reason to care. "Early shift," she said, then, looking for a way to add something honest, added, "I actually walked down here. I like walking."

Jack raised his eyebrows and asked her wasn't it a little cold for such a long walk.

Without planning to, she had moved closer to him, so that their arms were touching. She liked looking at him, and how strangely gentle he was. Leaning in and lowering her voice, she asked, "Are you concerned?"

Then, more explicitly than Annie thought was possible in real life, he looked her over, head to toe, and said, "You look like you know what you're doing."

For a moment she felt insulted—she was sure he was making a joke, mocking her age and awkwardness, how ridiculous she looked play-ing floozy in an unpeopled, unsexy bar. But he was smiling at her still, warmly, not derisively. Maybe she was someone worth look-ing at that way, in this setting, away from the utilitarian stupor of the Pages bookshelves or the evening exhaustion of her living room. Or maybe this had nothing to do with her—maybe he wasn't even really looking, just using his eyes the way they'd been trained to see women. Either way, she couldn't analyze away the warm feeling he'd dispensed on her with his once-over.

Jack nodded at the bartender as he brought their drinks. No money was exchanged. She thought she caught the bartender cast an extra parting glance between the two of them. She had that feeling again, that this had happened a thousand times before: this exact interaction, maybe even with this same man. The only new thing was her.

"You have," he said, raising his glass, "a New York sense of adventure."

That made her smile. She'd always thought that was one of her better qualities, but Paul had never appreciated it. "It's cheaper than an African safari," she said.

Jack breathed silent laughter of approval. He asked her if she'd always lived here.

"Born and raised."

"That's a surprise," he said. "I figured only a tourist would wander into a dump like this." The words sounded like a joke, but his face told her he was serious. He looked genuinely sad. It was as if someone had turned off the lights and left him there.

He wasn't menacing or creepy, but at that moment she felt pity for him, which amounted to the same thing. She didn't want what she was doing to feel depressing. When Jack hung his head and lost his posture, the bar looked dirtier, the lighting dimmer. She had to change this, now, or get out altogether.

"Does that mean you're not from around here?" she asked, lifting her shoulders, urging her breasts to come along.

"No. I've been here my whole life too. But..." he looked around despondently, like a lost child, then concluded, "this place suits me."

She affected a cute little frown and asked, "And it doesn't suit me?"

That seemed to snap him out of it. He showed her another version of his smile, this one even more straightforward than his once-over. "You're a girl," he said, "for one."

She smiled back at him, trying to mirror his expression. "Thanks for the drink."

The cider was sweet, more juice than alcohol. She loved it. She could probably get drunk this way, without noticing. That's how she'd want to do it.

"So," he said, angling himself towards her slightly, "what do you like to do, besides walk?"

Annie took a big swallow of cider, then shook her head. "That's it! That's really... no, I'm not kidding, that's it, that's all I do, I walk." She laughed, more, she knew, than was appropriate for what she had just said, but it really did strike her as funny. "Day and night," she added, which made her laugh more.

When she looked at Jack, he had a warm, surprised smile, appreciating the strangeness of her and her enjoyment. The smile kicked her in the stomach. Something felt horribly unfair. She felt tears poking out. "Stop," she said involuntarily.

"What?"

"Nothing. Sorry, nothing." She sniffed and took another big gulp of cider.

He wasn't smiling anymore, which was fine with her. "Are you OK?"

She realized then, for the first time in her life, that she hated nothing more than men asking her if she was OK. She could take everything, anything else, all of it, if she never had to hear that again.

"I'm—"

Saying "I'm fine" to the men who asked her this question was her second most hated thing. She grinned at him instead, and hoped that would suffice. It did. He changed the subject, and she loved him for it.

"Where's your favorite place to walk?"

"I don't really have one. You just sort of start out from wherever you are, and go from there. And you find new places along the way, places you maybe haven't seen before. That's the best part."

He nodded and drank his drink, as if he was absorbing something profound. "OK," he said, "so what's your favorite place you've found, on a walk?"

She had to think about that for a minute. Jack seemed to appreciate her need to reflect, and stayed quiet.

"The handball courts," she said, after a good silent moment had passed. "In Chinatown on the East Side, below Delancey."

She hadn't been to the handball courts in years. She remembered that a couple big busy streets parted and made way for them in a central plaza, and that it reminded her of the park on Houston next to Sunshine Cinema, in that way that New York echoes itself in different parts of the city and across the boroughs. Without knowing anything about handball, she could tell that the players in this park were not amateurs; there seemed to be an order to the play, a system. She imagined this was a place people came every day.

What she couldn't remember was where she was in her life when she found the handball courts—which apartment, which job, which boyfriend—and she knew that that missing piece was important, because it would have changed the way she'd see them. Finding them on that day would have filled some need or solved some problem. Her life used to happen in stages, like moving from grade to grade in school; she'd lose a job or a boyfriend and that, without much warning, was the new stage: a new set of people and places. Even loneliness could feel new, although it never was. She used to find that impermanence comforting, even liberating. The shifts were sudden and usually not her choice, but they were still a relief.

She didn't say any of this to Jack, but he was looking at her, Annie thought, like he had read at least some part of it on her face.

"I don't know why I like it there," she said.

"You just do," Jack said, and looked at her. "That's the point of those kinds of places. Right?"

The bar around them was quiet. A generic classic rock song that seemed to have been going on forever was playing softly on the jukebox. Annie hated songs that were longer than five minutes.

"Yes," she said, "that's right."

The two other guys at the middle of the bar were settling up and pulling on their coats. Annie watched them go. Neither of them was bad-looking. One of them reminded her of someone, but she couldn't think of who it was. If she had made one small decision differently, she'd be with them now, instead of Jack.

"Want another drink?"

For a second she wasn't sure who Jack was talking to. She'd finished the cider, without noticing. "You're going to buy me another drink?"

He laughed. "Sure, why not. I don't usually have someone to buy drinks for. Makes me feel important."

She knew he meant it as a joke, but she found the sentiment touching. "I don't usually have someone buying drinks for me," she said. "Go ahead."

Jack caught the bartender's eye, nodded and pointed to their empty glasses. Annie was embarrassed at how cool she found the whole thing. It was like they had their own secret language; like a speakeasy!

They shared their second drink in silence. She let herself start feeling fuzzy, slowly, and felt far away from everything. Jack had lived here all his life, too, and she'd never seen him before, and would probably never see him again. What an incredible city. Or, she realized, he'd been lying about where he was from, and that, in a way, was incredible too.

With each passing moment, it felt more OK to let the quiet keep going. Neither of them was supposed to be doing anything. Neither of them could possibly disappoint the other one, because they didn't know each other.

After a while, Jack said, "I think I'm going to head out." She'd only drunk half of her cider but he'd finished his drink, and she was full anyway.

She nodded. "You too?" he said.

Annie nodded again. "Yeah. Yes, me too."

Just outside, he pulled her to him and kissed her. She was overwhelmed by the warmth and heft of it, the soft pressure of his big chest and arms. That part felt good; her instinct was to sink into it. Then she felt the liquored heat of his mouth, and she liked something about that too, so she didn't stop him right away, but after a few seconds the taste settled in and made her step back from him.

She saw Paul then, in his purple chair. He was reading the paper; then he put it down, and saw the two of them, and smirked at her. Not at Jack; right at her.

She made a little noise like she was about to spit something out. Jack looked like she'd hurt his feelings; like no one ever had before this moment. A part of her wanted to push past the discomfort and kiss him again. Mostly, though, she wanted to be far away from him and never see him or think about him again.

She wanted to say "I'm married," but it came out "I'm sorry." He asked something about cab fare or at least walking her to the subway and she was already walking away from him, quickly, as she declined, tossing out a couple more apologies as she went. She didn't want to go anywhere else with him. She didn't want him to exist anywhere but on this block, in front of this bar, and if this block disappeared, all of it, the pavement and the awning and the stupid Guinness sign creaking and flapping endlessly above his head as he grew smaller and farther away, she wouldn't mind that either.

16

It was late. Annie wasn't home yet and she hadn't called, but Paul wasn't worried, just feeling guilty for not worrying. He couldn't even manage to stay up while he waited; he fell asleep shortly after he put Thomas to bed.

The noise that woke him was unfamiliar, but he knew right away that it was serious. The sounds of a house are predictable; they don't change, no matter how much a nighttime imagination attempts to transform them into something sinister. This was a foreign rustling, and it was coming from Thomas's room, accompanied by whimpering little-boy noises he hadn't heard since before Thomas could speak. The noise wasn't that loud, really, but the fact that it reached him from the other room made it feel urgent: this was one of those moments, he thought, when a parent's animal instincts kick in, when people become supernatural.

What time was it, he wondered as he walked through the dark, and where was Annie? For a moment, something occurred to Paul that made him choke on air—it was happening. He hadn't asked her about it, and now it was happening, and what he would see when he went into the next room would scar him so badly that he may not be able to pick up his life again from that point, and they'd become one of the families he'd read about, one of those stories that sounds made up, that you pray, God willing, will never happen to you...

But she wasn't there. Thomas was alone in his bed. Paul was so relieved he didn't care that she still wasn't home; wherever she was, anywhere was better than in this room with their son, bringing forth these noises.

His small body was moving under the covers, twisting in all directions with such determination that it looked like he was being pulled by invisible hands. Paul walked to the head of the bed, so that he was standing over Thomas—his face was contorted in a frightening grimace, his eyes squeezed shut with what looked like great effort and his little mouth open just enough to let out a staggered whine, like someone was hurting him with rhythmic regularity, like whatever it was fed off the sound of his pain.

It was hard to see him like this, but he was still mostly relieved from the ebbing away of the surge of adrenaline he'd felt before. As if in response, Thomas's whines climbed to a new intensity, and he tossed his limbs around as if possessed.

Paul found a place where his son's flailing body would let his arm in, placed his hand on Thomas's shoulder and shook him with the practiced gentle touch he'd learned from waking Annie mid-walk. Nothing happened; if anything, the outside force gave the boy's body momentum and stirred him up more. Paul hated the idea that he'd somehow made his son's nightmare worse, that he might be an active part of whatever imaginary thing was chasing or threatening him. He moved from a shaking to a smoothing, rocking motion, hoping it might have a calming effect. Thomas continued, as if his father wasn't even there, kicking his legs and whining in rhythm with the gentle rocking.

Paul stayed there for what felt like a long time, not knowing what else to do. If he went back to bed, he'd only stay awake, listening to Thomas and feeling worse.

At some point, the whines became less frightening; then, eerily soothing. Paul felt himself nodding off, and wondered what it would look like to Annie, him perched above their son, asleep, his hand anchoring the boy's shoulder as he writhed around in unseen torture. What woke him was a sudden stillness as Thomas finally came to rest. Paul barely had time to register the change, though, because as soon as he'd stopped moving, Thomas sat straight up and screamed.

He had never heard a sound like this before; certainly not from Thomas, and maybe not from any human being. The noise was high and gravelly, like it was being dragged over rocky terrain on its way out of the boy's body, and it seemed to be coming from every part of him. It was like hearing his son's insides, like they'd worked their way out of him and now they were here, alive, pumping, with nowhere else to go.

"Thomas," he said, frantically smoothing his son's sweaty bangs out of his eyes and rubbing his back, which felt like it was on fire. "It's OK now. I'm here. I'm here, sweetie, it's OK."

Thomas didn't even blink. He continued to scream with the resolve of a siren, without so much as a breath for air. If he recognized his father, or even knew he was there, he wasn't showing it.

Paul tried to shove away the word which surfaced for the second time that night: his son seemed possessed. He didn't believe in anything like that, and he wanted to trust his beliefs over everything else now, even the things he could see and hear and touch, but ultimately he knew it was stupid to really believe in anything anymore.

Paul was crying now, and it seemed the only word he knew how to say was his son's name, which he repeated over and over again. He held the boy's screaming face to his chest, which only muffled the noise. He held him there and rocked back and forth, the two of them in a single motion, like war widows holding their children's remains. *What else?* the rocking asked of no one in particular. *What else can I do?*

Then there it was, unmistakable: the unlocking of the front door. The noise woke Thomas up; he sat up in his father's arms, looking at him with that blank smartness, so familiar and, at this moment, so completely wrong. "Dad?"

"Thomas! God, you're OK..." Paul realized after he said it that it would make no sense to him. Of course he was OK; he'd been there with him the whole time.

Thomas touched three fingers to his voice box. "My throat hurts," he said.

"I know." Paul moved his arm from behind Thomas and lay him back down. He could feel the helpless panic draining away, as his parenting confidence filled back in. "You were just having a bad dream, old pal. It's over now, and you can go back to sleep."

Thomas shook his head. "I didn't have a dream."

"It's OK, Thomas," he said, easing himself up from the bed. "Sometimes we don't remember our dreams. It happens. From what it sounded like, it's just as well that you don't remember that one anyway."

He shook his head again. "No, Dad, I'm telling you I didn't have a dream. I know sometimes I forget, but I didn't forget, because when I forget I always at least remember some of it. I didn't have a dream." He sat back up, as if he'd just remembered something. "What do you mean, from what it sounded like?" His eyes darted around the room, as if he thought someone might be hiding in the closet. "What are you doing in here, anyway?"

I just want everyone to be asleep, Paul thought. *It's whatever the fuck o'clock in the morning. Why can't we all just be asleep?*

"You were—" he began. "I just wanted to check on you, old pal," he said, backing towards the door. "Get some sleep now."

He left Thomas's door open, fully aware that the light from the hallway was shining right in his face.

Annie knew that post-midnight was too late for her to be getting home. Paul would be unhappy with her; he'd ask her where she'd been, she'd tell him the story she'd practiced in her head on the subway, with any luck he'd buy it, and it would be over.

She crept up the stairs slowly, measuring each part of her foot on each step, a teenager again, thinking the same sneaking-in-late thoughts: *Maybe he'll be asleep. Maybe he won't even know. Maybe this will never come up, ever.*

Then, another familiar feeling: all that effort, the ridiculous tiptoeing, only to find him awake in their bed with all the lights on, staring at the ceiling, waiting for her.

It's going to be OK, she mentally intoned. *This is what I prepared for.*

"Hi," she said, and Paul turned at the sound of her voice. The expression on his face suggested that he hadn't even noticed she'd been gone, which Annie took as a calculated insult.

"Oh," he said, "hi." She waited in the doorway for him to say more, but he didn't. This was a new option, an infuriating, unexpected one: maybe he didn't care.

She decided to go about her nighttime business; since he wasn't giving her any reason to believe he was upset, she had no reason to stand on ceremony. She knew she should be relieved as she undressed and pulled her nightgown on in what should have been refreshing silence, but she felt annoyed, and hurt. There certainly wasn't anything unusual about her husband ignoring her, or treating her like a weirdo after a certain hour, but that had changed recently, if only for a couple weeks. It felt like longer. It had certainly been long enough that she missed it now.

"Can I ask you to do me a favor?" he asked while her back was turned to him. She turned around to find him still staring at the ceiling. Something in his voice made her feel like a sounding board, like she could have been anyone. Now she was almost certain that he hadn't noticed how late she was. "Do us a favor, really," he continued, clearly working out whatever this was in his head as he went along.

Annie nodded, though she knew he wasn't looking at her. Another teenage game was attempting to make herself invisible by speaking as little as possible.

"Can you ask Dr. Schecter—"

"Scheckman," she corrected automatically. She was surprised to discover that she took the mistake personally. Maybe it was just that thing people say about lying, that someone who's telling the truth will make mistakes, but a liar, who depends on their story, will get the details right every time.

"Right, Scheckman. Can you ask him about Thomas?"

"Ask him what?"

"Thomas—" Paul trailed off and played with his hands. Now Annie really didn't understand what was going on. The way he was fumbling around and avoiding her eyes, you'd think he was the one who'd just walked in after midnight.

Finally, he looked at her, for the first time that evening. Heat flooded her cheeks. She was sure that however her face looked would betray everything, that Paul would forget whatever it was he was about to say and figure it all out. "I think they're called night terrors," he said. "I went in there because I heard him making noise in his sleep, and when I got there he was tossing and turning and for a while he wouldn't wake up, and then when he did he just screamed and screamed, like he didn't even recognize me, then when you came home he just sort of snapped out of it and he didn't even remember that he'd had a dream at all."

Annie tried to piece together what her husband was saying, but the meaning of his words was overwhelmed by the urgency with which he delivered them, like a child recounting a playground fight. He looked like a child, too, helpless and scared.

Before she could register what he'd said about Thomas and attempt to tackle what Dr. Scheckman might have to say about it, Paul composed himself and went on; she thought of a little kid wiping his tears and snot away with the back of his sleeve. "Night terrors," he said. "I think that's what they're called." He took a moment, maybe to recite the words over to himself, then gave a determined nod to no one in particular and turned back to her. "So," he said, any trace of fear now gone, "can you ask him about that?"

"Sure," she said. "But… you think this might be related to me? To my—" One thing Stephen Scheckman hadn't changed was how nervous they both still were to actually say the words. She imagined Scheckman would probably advise her to stare it down, be direct, call it by its proper name. But maybe they hadn't covered that yet. "I mean, you want me to ask about it that way?"

Paul shook his head; he moved his shoulders and arms, too, like he was trying to wrestle off a bad memory. "I don't really know, Annie. He's the doctor, right?"

She slid in next to him, under the covers. "Right," she said.

They sat next to each other in silence for a moment; for once, Annie couldn't label the silence as good or bad. So often lately it was clear that what was taking up space between them was something ugly and powerful. Now, she was just waiting for him to speak.

She was exhausted all of a sudden. After she left Jack, she'd walked around for a long time, too wired to retreat to the subway and go home. The walk didn't calm her down; from the time she left the bar until this moment, she'd been jumpy and nervous, and wide awake.

It took her a moment to realize that Paul was crying. "Hey," she said quietly, and couldn't come up with anything more.

She'd only heard him cry once before, the day the towers fell. Fortunately, it happened on her day off, otherwise she would have been trapped in Manhattan. She hardly ever watched TV during the day, but she'd flipped it on that day, for some reason, as she vacuumed the living room carpet. It was the first thing she saw, that image that seemed almost unimportant now, so easy to call up and replay, but which, at the time, was still new, still impossible to see, almost beautiful, plucked from a collective nightmare. She'd called Paul downstairs and they'd sat there, like everyone else, watching, dumbfounded. She couldn't be sure, but vaguely recalled that they held hands.

At some point Paul announced that he was going to get Thomas from school and bring him home, and stood up in such a daze that, as she watched him go, she wasn't sure he'd remember how to get there. She was alone then, probably only for about thirty minutes, but it felt like days. There was no one to tell her that the nightmare wasn't coming true, that she wasn't, as she'd always suspected during the worst hours of the night, the last person left on Earth; that this wasn't what it had come to.

When she'd heard the front door open, she realized she'd forgotten to lock it behind her and for a moment had the ludicrous thought that someone might be breaking in. When her husband and her son walked in, she felt overwhelmingly grateful—not happy, she remembered, but grateful, a much less frivolous emotion. She couldn't stand up; she only extended her arms and they came to the couch to join her, and stayed there for the rest of the day, watching in silence, holding each other, none of them saying anything because they knew that being there was all they could do.

At some point they ate; at some point they put Thomas to bed, sitting there and watching until he fell asleep the way they used to when he was an infant, because all of a sudden it seemed necessary again. When they walked back downstairs, Paul turned off the TV and she didn't argue. They went to bed shortly after that, holding onto each other, waiting to wake from the dream, feeling the weight of adulthood, knowing that they were supposed to know better but couldn't, not today.

And she hadn't cried, but he had, all day: silently, as they watched the footage, his shiny cheeks communicating what none of them could; and later, in bed, physically and audibly, trembling against her side as if she was his protector, when really she felt like she would never be able to protect anything again.

Everything from that day was unclear in her memory; it could have happened in any order, and she might have erased whole portions or added parts that hadn't actually taken place. The only thing she was sure of was that as they lay in bed, Paul told her he was sorry. He'd gulped back tears and pulled away from her so that he could say it to her face, as if it was a crucial message, as if it made any sense. What could he possibly mean? she'd wondered as she cradled his head against her, saying nothing.

Now, he was on the other side of the bed, which continued to feel further and further away. The difference between then and now was that this time, she hadn't been there. He's crying, she thought, because he thinks he's alone.

"You're not alone," she said out loud, and even though it didn't really make sense, he nodded and moved closer to her.

Maybe he'd been remembering that night too, because he wrapped his arms around her and ducked his head into the same position. Just like that, it made sense again.

This time, though, he didn't stay that way. He began to move his hands up and down the length of her nightgown, then eventually slid them up under the hem. At first she was nervous that he would sense something, somehow, a foreign scent or something even less tangible, that this would erupt into some French bedroom drama of betrayal, but Paul didn't say anything, and he fell back into their old sequence of movements so easily that eventually she just let him go, and even managed to relax a little. She hadn't realized until now how long it had been.

There was nothing special about this time—it wasn't a rekindling or a passionate dam bursting—but it was familiar, which was enough to make her sad. For the stretch of time that Paul was close to her like this, she felt safe, and she had stopped hoping that she'd feel that way again. For the tiniest moment, she felt a rebirth—a miracle. It was only when he pulled away from her, and a look passed between them in the space where a kiss should have gone, that she remembered it wasn't real. It was only a dam bursting.

When they were finished, he rolled back over to his side of the bed, which seemed to have moved another two feet away. He looked at her sideways. "You're home kind of late," he said.

She couldn't remember any of the things she'd planned to say on the subway. It felt irrelevant now, like she could tell him the truth and it wouldn't even matter. "I went to a movie," she said.

The room was silent for a long time. When she looked back at him he was facing away from her, his body still. "I need to get some sleep," he said.

She was naked, and wide awake. "Good night, Paul," she said, then spent what felt like hours waiting for him to answer until she eventually fell asleep.

17

Paul's instinct the next day was to indulge his sleep crime obsession, but found that it made him too upset. He couldn't concentrate on work either. He stared at his screensaver—pleasant pastel shapes swirling over each other in a rhythm and pattern calculated to look spontaneous. It wasn't until someone knocked on his office door that he realized he'd become momentarily hypnotized, and had all but forgotten where he was.

He was even more confused when he looked up to find Kathy Burke standing in his doorway, since this was how his fantasies often began: interrupting him from some menial task with a flimsy excuse to stand there, for an unnaturally long time, perfectly framed by the door so that he could observe the exquisite paradox that she was. Her outfit today was as somber as ever, a tweed jacket and skirt over brown stockings and awful shoes that looked like what a colonial Puritan might wear to a wedding, but her hair was straight out of a love-in—long, dark, thick and unkempt, fanning out on either side of her face with no regard for fashion's demands for shine and restraint. Her face was a hybrid of the two worlds: a severe jawline and long nose, almost too long, but warm blue eyes and that smile, always so calm, that he liked to think she saved just for him.

"Paul," she said, "hi. Am I interrupting?"

Am I interrupting? It was as if she was auditioning for his porn screenplay.

"No." He planted his hands palms-down on the desk, resisting the urge to formally stand up to greet her. She probably just wanted to borrow paper clips or something.

She shuffled further into the room, still hovering by the doorway, not really within distance of intimate human contact. Paul wondered if she was shy, maybe, or just coy. He felt a stir and hoped to God he wouldn't get an erection. "Please tell me if I'm imposing," she said. "I just wanted to make sure everything was OK. With you, I mean."

"OK? With me?" He had no idea what she was talking about. Paul was a locked vault at work; he wasn't even sure his coworkers knew he was married, or that he had a kid. There was no way he could have possibly even hinted at his family problems to anyone.

"It just seems like you've been around a lot less," she said. "I feel like you've been leaving early during the week, or at least your office has been empty. And I know it's really none of my business, but we don't exactly have a warm and welcoming faculty around here—I mean, the environment can be quite cold, I find, so I just wanted you to know that if there's anything going on that's causing you stress, maybe it's spilling over into your work, maybe not, but that if there's anything you need to talk about—" She stopped herself, caught her breath, and smiled sheepishly. "Well, you should talk about it. That's all."

Paul's mind raced, and the stirring did not subside. She noticed his absence. She walked by his office, looking for him. She missed him when he wasn't there. *During the week*—it was only Mondays and Wednesdays, but to her it felt like every day, because every day she couldn't see him was agony. No one had sent her, no one had put her up to it, this was human interest, pure and simple, one person reaching out to another, needing him, aching to know the content of his mind and his heart...

She'd psyched herself up for this conversation, he was sure of it; she'd walked down the hall then turned around, debating, turning it over and over in her mind, should she, shouldn't she, no of course she shouldn't, he was a married man and what would he think, oh stop being ridiculous of course it was fine, he'd never suspect that's what she meant, not yet anyway, and what if he felt the same way, what if it did lead somewhere and he told her that yes, thank God you're here, please let's go get a cup of coffee and I'll tell you everything I've been wanting to say but no one would listen, not until now, not until you, Kathy... It did happen, he imagined her telling herself. You did hear stories of people leaving their wives for other women, women who understood them better, women they didn't marry just because it seemed like a sensible idea at the time. She was here, in his office, opening herself up to him, and this was the first day of everything.

"Well," he said, trying to shape a smile that was genuine, off-the-cuff, irresistible, "that's very considerate of you, Kathy, thank you. Very sweet. The truth is—" Was he imagining it, or did he see her lean in towards him, slightly, when he said that? "The truth is I have been a little delinquent this semester, it's true. My wife has a yoga class on Mondays and Wednesdays, she absolutely insisted that she needed this particular yoga class for the good of her sanity, and, by extension, mine and my son's, so I have to leave early to be with him."

Kathy nodded. He watched her for some sign of a heart breaking, or at least disappointment. If it was there, she hid it well. "Hey," he added quickly, "thank you for checking in, though. Really. You're right, this is not the friendliest work environment, and it's nice to have these little reminders that there are some human beings around."

She nodded. "I'm glad you understand."

"Believe me," he said, "I understand. And listen—" She was listening. He had her captive. He could say whatever he wanted. "I haven't mentioned these early escapes during the week to anyone; I know they're not a big deal, but people around here seem to have a remarkable knack for blowing things out of proportion. So..." More than anything, he wanted to find a way to say *our little secret*, but he couldn't bring himself to do it. He left his sentence unfinished, hoping that maybe she'd complete it with those exact words, and give him something to remember for nights and nights and nights to come.

Instead, she nodded and pulled her fingers across her lips, zipping them shut. Like they were in the third grade.

"Well," she said, drumming her hands on the door frame, "that's it, then. Have a good night. Stay warm."

He watched her tweed body moving away under the thick floating wings of her hair. Her parting words confused him, until he looked out the window and saw the few fat snowflakes that had begun to fall. He couldn't remember the last time he'd noticed the weather.

PART II

The Little Indian

18

"Hey, old pal," his dad said, looking at him in the rearview mirror. "Are you going to wear that thing all the way to New Hampshire? It's a long ride."

Thomas crossed his arms over his chest, like a real Indian. Native American. He couldn't remember which was the good one and which was the bad one—Miss Ackley had been very serious when she told them that there was one you should never say, and now he'd gone and mixed them up. He knew he looked a little funny like that, with his construction paper headdress and his arms crossed, but he didn't mean it as a joke. He hoped his parents knew that.

"Thomas," his mother said, "get this out of your system now, OK? Your dad's family isn't going to tolerate this the way we will." She sounded tired, but she was tired all the time. Thomas felt like he never saw her anymore. On Mondays and Wednesdays, she'd get home after he was already asleep; the rest of the week, whenever he saw her she was silent and nodding. She'd listen to him tell her what happened at school and nod, sit through dinner listening to him and his dad talk and nod, then before he knew it she'd be kissing him goodnight and he wouldn't be sure if he'd heard her speak all day.

Thomas was worried, but he was mad too. He'd try to find out what was wrong, but whenever he asked her she just smiled and shook her head, and sometimes she'd say, "Nothing, sweetie."

He needed her now, because he was still mad at his dad, who'd begun acting all weird and worried around him. He'd even stopped giving him Awesome Lessons. Now that he thought about it, his dad was quieter, too. Sometimes, on the evenings when they were alone, he'd look up from playing with his trucks on the carpet and his dad would be staring at him, with his hand over his mouth, hiding a weird smile. Once Thomas thought he even saw tears in the corner of his dad's eye. As soon as he saw that, he'd gathered up his trucks and went to his room. He had enough kids at school looking at him like he was a weirdo; he didn't need the same thing from his dad, too.

At least his dad had stopped waking him up in the middle of the night, insisting that he'd been screaming. That had been really annoying. He was so annoyed about that that he purposely didn't tell either of them about waking up sometimes on his own, how his throat would hurt worse than it ever had, burning like fire, how he'd feel sweaty and terrified and he wouldn't know why. Nighttime was really, really bad now, actually, worse than when he was having the airplane dream. He used to think that everything would be OK as long as his parents came in and hugged him back to sleep, but now he wasn't sure that would do anything. He didn't know how these things were going to go away, or if they ever would. He was starting to think maybe even grown-ups wake up scared in the middle of the night, and when that happens, who's there to help them?

He couldn't believe that a couple weeks ago he'd actually been excited about Thanksgiving, staying in that big creaky house that was always cold and always felt empty. There was nothing exciting about Grandma, who only liked him when he was quiet, and Grandpa, who was too tall for someone so old, and stared down at him wherever he went like he couldn't quite remember who he was. This year, his uncle Joe would be there, too. Thomas had never met him; all he knew was that his dad didn't really like him, but he didn't know why.

Ingrid was having two Thanksgivings. Her dad was taking her to his family's house in New Jersey, and her mom was just going to take her out someplace nice for dinner. When Thomas asked if she thought it was going to be weird, she said that all year everyone had been extra nice to her, like any minute she might start crying, and that she was pretty sure that Thanksgiving would be even more like that.

He kept his arms crossed and looked out the window. His headdress wasn't going anywhere.

His parents were monsters right now, he was sure of it. They'd found good disguises for the backs of their heads and the sides of their faces, but whatever he couldn't see was all fangs and yellow eyes. Their jaws snapped hungrily and saliva hung from their open monster mouths. It must be driving them crazy, Thomas thought, being so close to me and not being able to turn around and take a bite.

It was a good time for a vacation, Annie thought, but not this vacation. Any trip that began with an interminable car ride through the gray stretches of the Northeast in November couldn't end well.

She couldn't sleep in cars, but she hardly felt awake. Dr. Scheckman was proving ineffective. She was walking again, almost every night. In her dreams, she was flying. It felt wonderful.

Twice Paul had found her, grabbed her arm with unnecessary force and shaken her awake, as if she'd deliberately done this and broken a promise. She'd awoken to find his face inches from hers, staring at her with unmistakable disappointment. How could he access that hateful look so easily, she wondered, only moments out of unconsciousness? It was as if that was how he thought of her as he slept.

Once, Thomas woke her up with his screaming. She remembered the panic in Paul's voice when he described the first night terror to her, but nothing could have prepared her for the sound. She was at the other end of the hall in the bathroom when it happened, staring at her dark reflection again. She walked past Thomas's room, expecting to see Paul there, trying to calm him down, but Paul had either worked up an immunity to the screaming or had willfully decided to ignore it that night, because Thomas was alone.

She'd approached his bed slowly, as if sudden movements might escalate him into an even worse state than the one he was in now, thrashing around in his sheets like a hooked fish.

At the edge of his bed, below his little kicking legs, she sat down. She didn't touch him or shush him for a while, just watched her son and wondered if this was really even something that needed to be stopped. Maybe it was a beautiful part of Thomas, a shining piece of his true self that, if he were an adult, some pigheaded partner would try to suppress.

As she watched him, she decided she had asked Scheckman about the night terrors, like Paul had asked her to, and that what he'd had to say was surprising, but very enlightening. "It's a little different with children," he'd begun.

For convenience's sake, her father stood in for Scheckman in her imagination. He was an older Jewish man, with smile lines around his eyes, a deep, hoarse voice, a paunch, and an unthreatening beard. Maybe a little over-educated, sure, maybe a little insular in the New York way Paul liked to bitch about, but well-intentioned, and quick to laugh at himself.

"Parents are naturally very concerned about anything that seems unusual in their children," the imaginary Scheckman had said, "and sleep disorders can fall into that, and some can seem quite scary. But we have to be very, very careful with children not to smother qualities in them that, while unusual, can be crucial to the development of a creative, unconventionally-thinking person. Too many parents make this mistake, unfortunately."

Annie had asked, she imagined, if he was describing a Mozart/Van Gogh/Einstein scenario; if a modern parent's protective instinct might have effectively neutered their genius? Scheckman had smiled appreciatively. That was exactly it, he'd said.

She didn't want to interfere at all; she wanted to spend as long as he had the energy watching her beautiful son express this part of himself to her, and feel some pride knowing that if this completely unique hidden piece of Thomas did come from some outside influence, it was her. Only when she realized that at some point Paul might come in, and God knows what he would say if he saw her just sitting there, did she touch Thomas's head and his arm, move closer to him and shush him.

That was all it took. He slowed down, a little machine running out of battery, and stopped. Annie felt a swell of love that, she had to admit to herself, she didn't usually feel towards him during waking hours. He'd expressed himself, through sleep, and now he was finished, and resting. There was absolutely nothing wrong with her son. With either of them.

Paul hadn't said a word about any of it; if he had been awake that night and knew she went in to see Thomas, he didn't let her know. She knew he was worried about what would happen on this trip, if her body would err in front of his family, cause some concern or some stir in the pristine Mayfield household. That he hadn't brought it up explicitly, she imagined, was a kind of challenge: didn't Scheckman have some advice on how to prevent the condition when one was away from the home? She returned his silence with silence, and secretly hoped she would walk while they were there. It would provide a much-needed break from what was sure to be a monotonous nightmare.

She looked at Thomas in the rearview mirror and found him staring back at her. The thick brown line of construction paper cutting horizontally across his forehead made him look like a different person: more serious, if that was even possible, and with more purpose. It was frightening—Annie was used to that by now, but this time the stare that met hers wasn't indifferent, but undeniably angry.

In spite of everything, Paul was excited to be going home for a while. He did consider New Hampshire that way—home—especially lately. He thought that New England was beautiful in the way beauty was intended. New Englanders were loyal to their landscape because it was constant and humble, clean and undemanding. In that sense, it was the opposite of New York, and the people who lived there.

Somewhere along the line, someone had decided that cold was difficult, that people should try to get away from it. Paul thought the real unnatural climates were Texas, Arizona, places where people trapped themselves in their houses and their cars and their malls for months at a time, unable to leave because of the heat-stroke-inducing air. During the cruelest cold months, the people of New Hampshire were still mobile. They bundled themselves up and ventured into their small, safe neighborhoods, waved to one another in the grocery store and commiserated about the weather. Towns were support networks. People knew each other;

they made other people's business their business. It was a way of life a New Yorker couldn't possibly understand.

He hadn't even been eager to move to New York for college, but he couldn't turn down Columbia, the only Ivy that accepted him. That was how his parents had put it: you *can't* turn this down. Paul feigned excitement as he went; he would have been content to stay in New England long enough to become an adult there, and to pursue one of the pristine intellectual girls he'd been awed by in high school.

He loved the mixture of toughness and humility that New Englanders carried with them. He loved the coast of Maine and Cape Cod and the Connecticut suburbs, with their unselfconscious mansions peeking out from behind mazes of topiary and driveways. He loved Boston—all of New England rallied around one small city, no matter how far it was from where they actually lived, and clung to it with a patriotic ferocity that reassured the people from these tiny, disparate, forgotten towns that they were a part of something bigger.

"Hey, old pal," he said, "tell Mom some of the stuff we learned about Tuftonboro in our Awesome Lessons."

In the rearview mirror he saw his son roll his eyes, something he must have picked up from his mother. This wasn't supposed to happen yet; he was supposed to have six or seven more years before his kid decided he was too cool to learn anything from him.

"Thomas, tell her about the library fair."

"You tell her about the library fair."

He looked sideways at Annie to see if she was as taken aback by the uncharacteristic nastiness as he was, and was pleased to find her looking back at him, her eyes wide. For a moment, he felt like a new parent again, negotiating unknown territory with her, his partner on this nearly impossible terrain. For what seemed like so long now, they'd been operating as independent agents, each tackling the business of raising their child from vastly different angles, hardly even checking in with each other. He missed those early days of collaboration, of toughing it out.

"Thomas was pretty excited about the library fair, when we talked about it earlier this week," Paul said, pretending to speak to Annie but directing his words to the back seat. "It's been a Tuftonboro tradition since the year the town was founded, which was when, Thomas?"

Silence. He felt like a TA again, sweating and stammering in front of a room full of freshmen who had no interest in chemistry and didn't even bother to be polite about it. "That's right," he said loudly, "1795." He'd hoped that might provoke a smile somewhere in the car, but Thomas was still scowling and Annie had slumped back into her former position, facing forward, lost in some private bubble of boredom or resentment or whatever the hell it was she felt these days.

"We went to the library fair every summer," he went on. He was pretty sure neither of them were listening, but the radio was off—somehow the idea of filling the car with music seemed even more uncomfortable than silence—so he figured he might as well listen to himself talk. "Our neighbor had a booth where she sold four different kinds of pies, the same every year: apple, blueberry, peach and boysenberry. Some of the boysenberries came from the patch between our houses, and I remember I felt famous just seeing them all baked and finished, being eaten by everyone in the town."

He noticed that Thomas was using his Sitting Bull pose as an opportunity to run his hands up and down his arms to warm himself. Paul turned up the heat; the fucking kid wouldn't even deign to ask him to do it. Eight years old and already mastering the art of the silent treatment. He could kill Annie for that, for spreading her mopey influence, poisoning their innocent boy against him.

"My mother never let us get the pies, though," Paul continued. "She'd say something like, 'If you boys want a pie, I'd be happy to bake one. There's no sense in wasting money on something we can make ourselves.' I think she was afraid we'd think our neighbor's were better than hers, because they probably were. Everyone said they were excellent pies."

Was Thomas's strange mood related to the night terrors? As far as he knew, Annie had yet to bring any of this up with Dr. Wonder-ful, which would at least give him some perspective on the situation, allow him to know if he was damaging his child when he was trying to save him.

"There was the book sale, too, of course. That was the main event."

Not that he had any faith left in this doctor, anyway. It had been almost a month, and Annie was still a zombie. Every time he found her that way, the same thought occurred to him: *this* is what divorce is for. This would stand up in court. No one could fault him for leaving under these conditions.

"I was always amazed by how they managed to have such a great selection of books every single year."

The day before, Kathy had poked her head into his office to ask him about his Thanksgiving plans. Since they were seeing his parents this year, and not Annie's, he hadn't mentioned her at all. For the past week he'd been kicking himself for bringing her up in their previous conversation. After all, there was nothing inher-ently unfaithful about erasing her from the world he presented to other people. "I'm going up to New Hampshire," he'd said. "My son gets a kick out of being in the country."

It couldn't hurt, either—he imagined the day when Kathy finally got up the nerve to kiss him, with a sudden fluid motion, forcing her-self into a momentum she couldn't pull away from. Eventually, she'd rest her head on his shoulder, her hands on his chest, and speak into his neck. "I'm so sorry," she'd say. "I know I shouldn't have done that, it's just—well, you haven't mentioned your wife in a long time, so I thought maybe—"

"The library fair's in the summer, of course," he said. Annie's eyes were closed, and Thomas was looking out the window. "So I guess there's really no point in talking about it now."

19

They stopped at Friendly's. Thomas thought it was silly to have a whole restaurant where all anyone wanted to eat was the ice cream, but going to Friendly's was, as his dad said, a tradition, whatever that meant. He guessed it meant that they had to do it, no matter what. Usually Thomas could manage to be happy to be there anyway because the kid's meal came with the Happy Ending sundae—it was supposed to look like a man's face, with Reese's Pieces eyes and a cone on its head, like a birthday hat. Whenever Thomas took the first bite, his dad would make a face like he was sad and grossed out and he'd say, kind of quietly, "That poor guy."

Thomas wore his headdress at Friendly's. Each of his parents tried once to get him to take it off, then they left him alone. Maybe they could see how serious he was about it.

Their waitress was a pretty teenager with blonde hair in a ponytail. Her name tag said "Jennifer." When she saw him, she smiled and said, "Well, looks like someone's ready for Thanksgiving!" Thomas smiled back at her; it was the first time he'd smiled all day, and it felt good. His parents looked embarrassed.

They didn't talk as they ate their food. His mom played the little wooden peg-jumping game over and over again, without once asking for his help. She was pretty good at that game, and she got better every time. By the time their food got there, she'd played two games where she only had two pegs left at the end. Thomas could tell she was really frustrated that she didn't get a perfect game in. It was kind of funny.

They all got ice cream; his dad's banana split and his mom's mint chocolate chip looked a lot better than his sad little sundae. He wondered how long he'd be trapped on the children's menu like this, unable to get anything else. The Friendly's kids' menu said it was for ages 12 and under. Four more years; that seemed like a long time.

He stuck his spoon into the pathetic man with no mouth, right between his brown eye and his orange eye, and waited for his dad to say something, but he didn't. Neither of his parents were even looking at him; their ice cream seemed much more interesting to them at the moment. *Well, good,* Thomas thought. *At least I can eat in peace.*

Thomas didn't ask how much farther they had to go. He didn't ask for an Awesome Lesson about ice cream, and his dad didn't offer. There were two other families in the restaurant, but they were sitting far away; where they were was behind a wall of quiet.

"I'm going up to pay," his dad said finally, after the check came. He stood up to go to the register. "I'll meet you at the car."

"Thomas," his mom said. He looked up from his empty Happy Ending sundae and saw that she was really looking at him. "Come outside with me."

He followed her outside. She walked around to the back of the car, which Thomas thought was strange. For a minute she just kind of looked around at the parking lot with her hands in her pockets. Then, without saying anything, she dropped down into a squat in front of him so that she was staring right into his face and grabbed his shoulders. "Thomas," she said, "please." Her voice was high and quiet and a little shaky. "I need you to—look, I don't mind the headdress, I really don't, just please." She was breathing heavily and her words were coming out fast. "I'm having—a hard time recently, because I—" She stopped in the middle of the sentence and closed her eyes and shook her head, then started over again. "No. Never mind. Forget I said that, but listen."

There were tears in her eyes now, and she ducked her head into her arm to wipe them. When she came back up her eyes were red and Thomas noticed, for the first time, how awful she looked. It was as if she'd gotten stuck transforming out of her monster self. It made him really sad, for some reason.

"This vacation is going to be—" She gulped, then closed her eyes hard, took a deep breath and opened them again. "—difficult. I think. So I really need you to be a good boy, OK?"

No one had ever told Thomas to be a good boy before. And *this vacation is going to be difficult*—he had no idea what that meant.

He heard the Friendly's door open, and saw his dad coming out, rubbing his hands together. His mom looked up; she'd seen him too. When she looked back at Thomas, her eyes were wide open and her mouth was a little bit open, too. Her hands felt tight on his shoulders. He just wanted to be back in the car.

Thomas pulled the headdress off.

"OK, Mom," he said, and she pulled him in close to her and kissed his cheek and whispered "thank you" into his hair. Then his dad honked the horn and she gave him a little push and they each went to their separate sides of the car and got in and pulled the doors shut behind them and they drove away.

20

Betsy Porter Mayfield looked like she'd always been sixty-seven. She didn't look like she was clinging to youth, or being dragged kicking and screaming into old age; she was graceful, easing into the present as if she'd never been anywhere else.

Betsy's hair was a deep, settled-in gray, enviably well-kept and displaying no indication that it had ended up here after a long life of more vibrant color. Her wardrobe was the same way: she wasn't resigned to that old-lady look that practically smelled of the end of life. Instead, her clothes were well-coordinated and looked expensive—soft pastels and earth tones that hugged her compact frame as if they had been tailored just for her.

Her mouth never moved more than an infinitesimal amount away from a neutral position. If she was happy, it was hard to tell; if she was displeased, a trained eye might observe her taut cheekbones flex slightly as she set her jaw, and her tidy crow's feet would huddle in around her gray eyes. She walked with her hands clasped together in front of her, and sat that way, too; it was as if her entire body conspired not to reveal too much. But Annie knew her mother-in-law well enough by now that she'd figured it out: when in doubt, and especially if Annie was around, Betsy wasn't happy.

She was standing in the driveway, waiting for them, when they pulled up. Annie sighed. So much for being able to take a moment to pull herself together before giving all control over to Mother Mayfield. She'd outsmarted Annie, parking herself there as if to say, "You're in my territory now."

"Where is he?" she asked, before Paul had even turned off the engine. "Where's my little man?"

Early in their relationship, Annie might have gotten a kick out of her mother-in-law's antiquated endearment; now, all she could think was that she'd spent eight years making a conscious effort not to use terms like "my little man" to refer to her son, and Betsy's seemingly benign cuteness was just psychological sabotage in disguise.

"Hi, Grandma," said Thomas. Betsy crouched by his door, waiting, then scooped him into her arms when he came out. Annie got out and stood next to them awkwardly. She felt like she was interrupting an intimate moment, until Thomas found her face with a pained look, pleading for help. Annie tried to smile at him, but she was sure she looked as frightened as he did. This was too close to a dream she'd had a couple nights earlier, where Betsy announced that Annie was unsafe for Thomas and that they were taking him away. She hadn't been able to say anything, only stare at the tire swing in the front yard of the New Hampshire house as it crept endlessly back and forth in a breeze that chilled her beneath the skin. She didn't like the way Betsy was holding him now, like Annie wasn't even there.

Since an acquaintance's politeness had crept back between them, Paul's family was off-limits as a subject of conversation, so she'd be alone on this trip with whatever thoughts she had about the Mayfields. At least she'd brought her journal; Dr. Scheckman would be proud.

Betsy stood up from Thomas's embrace and moved right into Paul's, keeping her back to Annie the entire time. "Mom," Paul said, endowing the syllable with a sentimental power Annie thought unnecessary.

She felt Thomas wrap his arm around her knees and pushed her fingers through his hair instinctively. This almost made up for everything else: her faux-pas with the mystery child on Halloween; Betsy's snatching him up immediately; even having to spend four days in New Hampshire. She felt her son breathing against her leg and looked at the White Mountains in the distance, imagining they were somewhere else, just the two of them.

It gave Annie a sense of supreme satisfaction that Thomas was still there when Betsy finally turned around to greet her. She felt an animal's possessiveness as she moved her arm down around his shoulder and tightened her grip, communicating to her mother-in-law, quite clearly, *Mine*.

"Annie," Betsy said, lifting her hands towards her like she was singing a national anthem. "Hello."

"Hi, Betsy." Reluctantly, she let go of Thomas to hug her mother-in-law. She felt small and skeletal in Annie's arms, like a bird. Betsy pulled away as if she were recovering from something unsavory.

At least, Annie knew, this would be the last of the embraces. Paul's father was not a hugger. She saw him when she looked back towards the house, leaning against the door frame with his arms crossed. His whole body didn't fit, so his head was slightly ducked, which gave him the unmistakable appearance of a vulture. Annie had run this theory by Paul before, and he'd responded with a silent shrug and a look that told her he'd taken offense.

"I didn't say he was *like* a vulture," she'd said, which was true: Victor Mayfield was not like a vulture. He was, in nearly every respect, like Frankenstein. He usually grunted in place of speaking and lurched around unsteadily, like a tree that had just grown legs. He towered over everyone and everything in his life and used his vantage point to scowl down at the world with a face that looked like it was carved out of wood.

Like Betsy, Victor's first priority was the child. He propped himself up from the front porch column and made his way down the stairs, his body jerking to the left and right with each staggered footstep. Betsy was facing away from her husband, but after fifty-some years of marriage she must have grown used to sensing his presence, because she backed away from the car to make way for him.

Annie imagined how Thomas's grandfather must look to him, standing a good four heads above him and looking down. She imagined the way his gray hand would grow enormous as it came closer to tousle his hair. "My boy," he said, his voice a growl so low it was almost a whisper.

Victor turned to Paul and nodded, once. "Son," he said. He shifted his eyes and repeated the nod towards Annie, this time without speaking. Annie almost smiled as the thought crossed her mind that he might have forgotten her name.

The silence that followed lasted only a couple seconds, but it was so painful that she immediately went to the trunk to get their bags, then brought them to the house, pulling Thomas along with her. *Let Paul stay with his family,* she thought. *Let them share this icy New Hampshire moment. We don't need to be here.*

The front door was open a crack. Annie pushed it the rest of the way with her shoulder. Her head was down, so she almost didn't notice the person who was coming out as she was going in. When the impact of another body made her look up, she saw someone she'd never seen before.

It took Annie a good ten seconds before she realized that this was her brother-in-law, Joe. When she finally found his name in her mind, she studied his face once more, for what seemed like the hundredth time in those few seconds, trying to place it in a memory, but came up blank. He'd been at their wedding, she knew for sure, but she couldn't find him there; there was only black and white and pink, flowers, pastries, and the infuriating sight of her mother crying. Her mind kept returning to the bar on 37th Street; the softness at the corners of his mouth and the broad, healthy frame that filled the doorway made more sense to her there than anywhere else.

She only knew him through layers of old photographs, half-told stories, and a name which had been repeated enough times that it had lost its meaning. He had never been real until now, and now he seemed too real to be true.

"Whoa," he said, stepping back slightly from the threshold of the door. "Careful." Then he smiled, which was chilling: his smile was identical to Paul's, formed the same way and revealing the same lips and teeth, but it was something she hadn't seen in a long time. It was like meeting a dead person in a dream.

Joe tilted his head, staring at the space to the left of her. Annie was confused at first; she'd forgotten she was still holding onto Thomas. "You OK, friend?" Joe asked.

Thomas nodded. He was no longer angry or frightened, but somber and open, the Thomas she knew. Maybe, like her, he sensed something good in this new person; maybe he could also barely contain his relief at being near a Mayfield who felt so different from the others.

"I'm Joe," he said, holding out his hand. "You must be Annie."

She'd met new people dozens of times in recent years, but at that moment it felt like the first time she'd ever had to react to a man who was offering his hand for shaking.

"Yes," she said, "I am." She held out her hand, mirroring his, then waited for him to meet her, which he did. It was less of a shake, she thought, than a hold.

He didn't let go, only pivoted his body around as he peered out the front door behind her. "Where's my big brother?" he asked.

Annie resented the tone of implied affection towards Paul. She wanted to tell him that his big brother wasn't looking forward to seeing him, that he didn't know anything about him—where he lived, what he was doing with his life—and didn't care. But she also knew that this was someone else's family. She was an outsider.

She wouldn't have thought it was possible for Joe's face to be any more welcoming, but as he looked past her into the front driveway, his eyes glowed and his smile broadened. She was losing him; how could any of those three people provoke that kind of reaction from someone who'd had to spend his entire life with them?

"Hey!" Paul said, coming up the steps behind her. Joe dropped her hand and walked past her shoulder to throw his arms around his brother in a man's embrace, all thumps and muscle. When Annie turned around, she expected to see Paul looking squashed and lost in his brother's arms, but instead he was grinning; he had the look someone should have when they're seeing a long-lost relative for the first time in years.

Before the two brothers could exchange any more words, Betsy was on the porch behind them, ushering everyone inside, out of the cold. Annie heard the words "freshen up" and something about dinner, and then everyone was disappearing to different corners of the house's vast interior. Paul was holding Thomas's hand and carrying his bag up the central staircase, an imperial affair with wide white steps covered in a rich green carpet. A few steps up, he stopped and turned around. "Annie," he said, "come on."

Annie turned in time to see Joe's back disappear towards the kitchen, on the first floor. She wondered if those couple of moments in the doorway would be the only time she'd be alone with him that weekend. Then she picked up her bag and followed her husband up the stairs to their room.

She spent most of dinner watching Joe talk to her son. He's an uncle, she tried to remind herself. He has no real responsibility. It's easy for him to act this way—to be so solicitous, to take in everything the kid says and respond thoughtfully, completely free of any ego, a blank slate, a man you could trust with anything. With your life.

Thomas was telling him about Ingrid and her two Thanksgivings. If he had been speaking to anyone else, Annie would have told him to give it a rest already. In the last week, any time Thomas wasn't pouting at them and administering the silent treatment with the resolve of a Benedictine monk, he was talking about that divorce, as if it was a trip to Disney World. She'd never liked the fact that he talked about Ingrid's parents with such reverence, like they knew something she and Paul didn't, like they'd figured out some life secret and were letting their son in on it when they occasionally had him over for quinoa salad or whatever it was they ate in their faux-enlightened bourgeois lair of bullshit. Annie wasn't even a little surprised to hear the news—Lydia was a spoiled, fake free spirit from Long Island and Daniel was a self-important literary agent, ten years older. It was probably doomed from the beginning, she thought, completely aware that someday soon, some backseat driver might just as easily reduce her marriage to a seven-word epitaph.

Eventually, Thomas ran out of steam, and the room was quiet. As if there was nothing left to say. *New England*, Annie thought. Betsy was all aprons and beneficence, smiling between her sons as if they weren't three seats apart, hardly making eye contact. They were emotional geysers compared to their father, though, who barely looked up, and gave new meaning to the expression "shoveling food into his mouth."

Annie stared down the side of Paul's face and hoped he might pick up a silent message from her, but he was as content as the rest of them to continue eating in a tomb. She was back in her own living room, carrying the crushing burden of sound.

"Joe," she said, "where are you living now?" *Where are you living now?* As if she'd ever known where he'd lived in the first place. Even now, she was working to save face for her husband, who would just as soon have gone the rest of his life without knowing.

Joe swallowed a mouthful of potatoes, a more delicate version of his father's horselike chomping. "Albuquerque," he said.

Albuquerque. She remembered her first date with Paul, when he told her he grew up in New Hampshire, how it had sounded like the same kind of music: unexpected, a place she might have forgotten about otherwise. It was as if that made him a better person than if he had said L.A. or Westchester, places she didn't have to leave up to her imagination. In the years that followed, New Hampshire had stepped out from behind the curtain of romance and revealed itself, gray and sickly, and Annie knew it would never go back to the mental postcard where it had lived before.

But, of all places, Albuquerque. Joe made sense all over again. There he was: halfway into the desert but still close enough to a main drag, where he had a favorite bar and a favorite taqueria. He'd picked up enough Spanish to exchange pleasantries with the owner. He took long drives; maybe sometimes he made it all the way out to Mexico on weekends. He taught in a school there, and the kids loved him; they called him "Señor Joe" and at recess they clung to his legs.

Paul's fork clinked on his plate. "So what are you doing these days?" he asked his brother. There was something mean in his voice, or maybe just a hint that he was irritated at having to ask. Annie kept her focus on Joe, gaining a new appreciation for the physical process of eating as she watched his jaw muscles churn and the veins in his neck pulse, then rest.

Joe smiled at Paul. "At the moment, odd jobs."

Something about the way Paul nodded, said nothing and went

back to eating made her determined to detach herself from her husband in Joe's mind. She tilted her head up and offered him a smile; she even batted her eyelashes a tiny bit.

If Joe noticed that, or the fact that his brother had checked out of the conversation, he didn't show it. "Carly's in school," he continued. "She's getting her master's in physical therapy." Paul looked up, puzzled, and Joe mirrored the expression. "I've told you about Carly, haven't I?"

Paul only shrugged. Annie knew that this was another jackass maneuver, but for some reason it didn't bother her as much this time.

"We met two years ago," he said, in a lilting voice meant to jog a memory. "We moved in together a few months ago. Didn't I mention her in my emails?"

Paul nodded, but it was like he was keeping time to music. "Sure," he said, "Carly. I remember."

Betsy's giddiness was tangible; it was as if she had been watching the conversation with the sound off. "My boys," she said. Annie thought it was one of the stupidest things anyone had ever said. "Who's ready for dessert?"

As she shuffled into the kitchen without waiting for a reply, Thomas asked Paul where Albuquerque was. Apparently, the war paint was off for good now, since he was back to using his father as his primary source of information, even if it was about someone else's life.

"It's in New Mexico," Annie answered, perhaps a little too loudly, before Paul could say anything. The three men looked up at her. The movement of her father-in-law's head reminded her of a cast-iron gate opening.

"Where's that?" Thomas asked, directing the question towards Paul again.

Annie answered again; she told him that it was as far away from here as you could possibly get without leaving the country. "Lemon meringue," Betsy said as she pushed through the swinging door, carrying an immaculate yellow thing on a platter.

She wanted to make the most of the close eye contact she and Joe were allowed after dinner, during the ritual good-nights. She wanted to communicate her disgust with her husband, and something about what she thought of him, and what she thought of Carly, who'd managed to ruin her evening from thousands of miles away. She wanted her eyes to do all that work; in movies, people did it all the time.

Instead, good night was just good night, and she couldn't even conjure up an imaginary significance from the look that passed between them. They were, after all, in a sterile land. It was hard to imagine so much as a fantasy passing between the cold walls.

In this house, sleep followed dinner. Thomas fell into step like an old pro, following his father up the stairs to their rooms in the most obliging, the most natural silence. The headdress had been vanquished by a little Puritan.

Paul fell asleep fast, or he did a good job of pretending. Annie intentionally forgot to write in her journal that night. There was only one thing she wanted to write about, in the grand tradition of every diary she'd kept since middle school: the discovery of a new boy. She doubted Paul would ever sink so low as to read the thing, but she couldn't risk it. That would really ruin things.

Annie stretched her legs out between the cold, crisp sheets. She hated to admit it, but she felt herself being pulled into sleep more easily than she had in weeks. This was a rooming house, after all, and it did achieve that anonymous, vacation-like quality of a hotel. Nothing was her responsibility here; she was being taken care of. The rest was out of her hands.

When she woke up, she was lying down, but something was still wrong. She wasn't where she'd been before. For starters, Annie was a back sleeper, and now she was on her side. She was also holding onto something—someone. Instinctively, she drew her arms back; Paul would wake up, find her there, and communicate in the least subtle way possible that she wasn't welcome within intimate range. But as she moved she felt the smallness of the body beside her, heard the high breathing and knew it was Thomas.

No panic set in; she did not rush to get back to her own bed before Paul discovered that she was missing. Instead she pulled her son closer, tucked her knees up to meet his. There was no need to go anywhere. This was where she should be. Her body, smarter than her at times, was trying to tell her as much, and she was willing to listen.

Annie didn't sleep. She listened to Thomas's breathing, felt its predictable rhythm against her. After remaining like that for a long time—ten minutes, an hour, it was impossible to tell this late—she was so attuned to his breath that she sensed the irregularity right away. It became shorter, quicker, like panting. Then she heard whimpers—tiny, quiet, but distinct. He was an animal in pain.

She stroked his hair and sent a long shush into the room; she didn't know if he could hear it, but she hoped he might sense it. It didn't help; if anything, he seemed to be getting worse. His legs thrashed as he began to move around in her arms. She loosened her grip, then let go of him completely.

Once she reached that point, simply lying beside him as he tossed and turned, it seemed pointless for her to be there anymore. Before she left, she touched Thomas's forehead, but he registered nothing. His face was tense with unflinching focus, concentrating on something she couldn't see.

21

In France, Paul found, daylight didn't appear until night was completely exhausted. You couldn't wake up late and comfort yourself, as he had done as a boy, with the purple strip of sky visible through his bedroom window that let him know the darkest part was over. In France, it was all black sky and piercing stars to the very end. It would have been romantic, Paul thought, to someone whose circumstances were even remotely romantic.

Paul couldn't remember the last time he'd walked alone this late at night. He'd imagined, when he told Annie he was going to get some air, that it would be liberating. He'd tried not to speculate about what it meant that she only shrugged and told him she'd probably be asleep when he got back. They'd been fighting, as usual.

The quiet was one Paul hadn't experienced before, a heavy silence that seemed almost to vibrate. He walked along the sunflower field which spread in every direction across the country road; during the day, it was radiant, cartoony in its yellow showiness. There were fields like this all over France; this was the height of the season, a hotel manager had told them.

Now, Paul could barely make out the outlines of the huge stalks. They'd ducked their heads in the sun's absence, and the field was just a void, taking up space. There was hardly any wind that Paul could feel, but the plants were more sensitive than him, and every step was accompanied by a rustling whisper, a movement he could only sense. There were probably small animals hiding there too, but he couldn't see them. He wished he could; it would have assured him that he was not the only living thing for miles.

When he stopped walking, it was because he felt he physically couldn't go forward anymore without knowing what was there.

There was nothing liberating, it turned out, about walking into darkness. He'd tossed himself into the wild, and all he had to do was turn around and walk back, but he couldn't do that either. His body wouldn't let him move.

He was at the edge of the road and the edge of the field, some distance away from the cottage; he didn't know how far. He didn't know how long he'd been walking. He put his hands in his pockets and planted himself there. He looked up. Stars; he'd come out to look at the stars. That was something people did, and it made sense, didn't it? They were the only light; where was the moon? Was there no moon in France? He let stupid questions roll around in his head for as long as they needed to as he stayed there, willing his body to adjust to the cold. His neck was stiff from looking up, but he adjusted to that too. At some point he fell asleep that way and woke up and nothing had changed, except that his body was ready to take him back.

He hadn't walked far; after only a couple minutes, the light shifted and the road opened up into the small parking lot outside the cluster of cottages. Paul stood for a moment and wondered what would happen if he forgot which one was his and wandered in to some other family. He thought of the folk tale about the foolish man who gets lost on a country road and ends up back where he started. Being a fool, he thinks he's in a new place, an alternate universe where everything is identical to his town—a wife who looks and speaks exactly like his wife, people who know his name and speak to him as if they know him. The fool decides to stay there, and lives the rest of his life thinking he's living in the bizarro world, but he doesn't mind. Paul didn't know if there was a specific moral to the story, but something about it had always appealed to him.

Inside there was more quiet, more dark. It was as if he'd brought the outdoors in with him—all of it: the vague rustling and the unseen wind, the road stretching for miles to the rest of Europe. There was something foreign here, too.

He felt for the door behind him, like in a dream, wanting to know that the solid world existed. Moments ago, he'd been asleep, on his feet, next to a field, in France. How could he be sure what was real?

Once his eyes adjusted to the dark, the first thing he saw was his and Annie's bed, its sheets rumpled and exposed. Empty.

His first instinct was to check on Thomas—he went over to the little bed and placed his hand in the vicinity of the pillow, his fingers tensed, only able to relax once he felt his son's hair and heard his breathing. He was relieved, enough to feel content just sitting on the floor next to Thomas, leaning against the bedframe.

Then, in what felt like a physical blow, he felt the full weight of his exhaustion. He wanted, he needed, to be asleep. He could, he realized, if he wanted to. If he didn't look for her right away, no one would know.

He'd wonder, later, whether he would have just left it alone if a noise hadn't startled him awake, doing the work for him. It came from the little kitchen alcove—Paul couldn't help but associate the word "little" with everything in the cottage; it made it seem cute, harmless, not quite real. Annie was there, in the dark, standing still and not speaking and holding something.

Of course. Just because, miraculously, it hadn't happened on this vacation, yet—he'd actually almost managed to forget that it had happened at all—didn't mean real life could just go away.

"Annie!" he whispered, though he might as well have been yelling, the way the word tugged itself from his throat, fast and ragged. "You OK?"

She still didn't answer.

He slid his feet across the cold tile floor the way he would as a child, trying not to make noise on the creaky wood floors. When he reached her, he touched her arm and said her name again.

She jerked at his touch; he felt her entire body move as it sprung away from him, and there was a noise that seemed to split the room in half. It was like a flash of light that disappeared immediately but left its residue behind, temporarily blinding him.

After her initial physical shock, Annie awoke easily, almost gracefully, opening her eyes as if she were being greeted by the sun after a restful night. When she turned to face him, her face implied a question, but she didn't say anything.

Paul found it difficult to look away from her, but something distant occurred to him and he turned around to look at Thomas's bed. He appeared to still be asleep.

When he looked at his wife again, it was easier to speak, though not to make sense of what was happening. "Annie, what—"

She didn't answer, but followed his gaze to the floor, where the knife had landed.

Annie opened her mouth. Somehow he knew she wasn't going to say anything, so he didn't give her the chance to. He walked back to the front door, and once he was outside he ran until he reached the rental car, then drove away.

It made sense to be in and out of sleep all night here in his parents' house, where, as a child, he sometimes spent entire nights awake. Every shadow on the wall reinterpreted itself as ghost or monster or lurking murderer. In those days, it was the product of a child's imagination, or so he'd thought.

What was David Stellar's wife thinking the night her husband mistook her for a nightmare? Had she been a sound sleeper as a child, or had she spent nights awake, fearing some danger she could sense years in advance? Shadows seemed like long-lost friends now, a welcome alternative to the real, inescapable fear of the person lying next to him, asleep for now, but for how much longer? And how could he expect her to do anything in this house she hated, half-woken from her undead sleep and angry at her surroundings, other than to let her unconscious guide her to the kitchen, to the knife drawer, to the sleeping forms of people who had no idea what someone with her condition was capable of, and, eventually, to him, stupid enough to believe that it couldn't actually happen?

What did his eight-year-old son see through his screams in the middle of the night? Thomas refused to tell him, to even acknowledge that it was happening, but maybe Dr. Scheckman would advise jogging his subconscious memory: "When you dream, do you ever see Mommy? What's she doing? Is it something scary? You can tell me, Thomas. It's OK. I see those things too."

He stretched his arms out and felt an out of place, transgressive freedom in his fingertips. Annie wasn't there. He closed his eyes, not like he was going back to sleep but like he had heard bad news. Irritating news. *Now this.*

He pulled himself up and tried to wake up his brain. He wasn't confident he could navigate the big house in the dark. What if he fell down the stairs and broke his neck hunting his crazy nightwalker wife? Should he bring a flashlight? Where the hell would he find a flashlight right now?

He started to walk into the hallway. Then a toilet flushed and the light in their bathroom went off.

"Jesus, Annie," he said, sinking his head into his hands as she emerged and came back to bed.

"What's with you?" she said, and he snorted a laugh in response.

He hadn't even gotten back into bed when the noises started from down the hall, where Thomas was staying. He was in the little room at the end where sad old men used to spend summers; they'd poke their turtle heads out for meals and then retreat. Paul used to wonder what they did up there all day, and the perspective of all these years hadn't given him an answer.

He heard Annie move next to him, starting to get up.

"*No,*" Paul said, with a force even he didn't recognize. "No. I'll go. Jesus. I'll go, I'll go." He threw the sheets up to the pillow on his side of the bed, as if that was a door he could lock to keep her down. "Fuck, Annie." He had to remind himself not to slam the door as he went out.

He managed to get to Thomas before any real screaming happened. *Thank God,* he thought, as he rocked him like a baby and felt his stirring body become more still. That usually worked.

Once he was asleep again, he laid him back down and arranged the sheets around him. His son opened one eye, suspicious as always, staring up at him like a little narc. "Dad?"

"It's OK, old pal. Go back to sleep."

"Dad," Thomas said again. "Are you OK?"

Paul hadn't realized that he was crying. "Yeah," he said, swallowing, gulping, pulling himself together. "Yes, kiddo, I'm fine."

He bent down and kissed Thomas's forehead. "I'm OK if you're OK," he whispered to his son. "Don't you know that?"

22

After a little while lying in bed, Thomas got up and got dressed. He looked at his headdress, which was sitting on the chair in the corner. He knew his mother had asked him not to wear the headdress anymore, but he was almost certain it had something to do with what had happened the night before: he'd seen his mom disappear.

Really, he'd seen her *as* she was disappearing. Thomas didn't exactly know the details of it yet; maybe she'd been on her way to disappear, or coming back from it, or right in the middle of it. All he knew for sure was that she had been in his doorway, and he'd tried to talk to her and she hadn't heard him, and after he'd tried again a couple times he'd realized what was happening. Then he'd waited for her to turn into a monster, but she didn't, and it made him happy. It made him so happy he'd gone back to sleep, knowing that something was different and really good. He hadn't decided yet if he was going to ask her about it; maybe that was against the rules. Secrets were complicated.

He put on the headdress and went downstairs.

He thought his mom would be upset when she saw him wearing it, but when he walked into the dining room, she looked up at him from the table and said, "Good morning, sweetie, how did you sleep?" He couldn't remember the last time she'd said that much to him while she was smiling.

Thomas didn't say anything, just adjusted the headdress and waited for her to say something about it, but she didn't.

Grandma Betsy came out of the kitchen, holding a plate of pancakes; every time he saw her, she was holding a plate of food, and every time she was holding a plate of food she looked happy. It was like magic: as soon as she put the pancakes down on the table, she frowned. "Well," she said, like a teacher waiting for you to tell them why you're about to get in trouble, "what is that?"

His mom answered before he could. "He made it in school." He waited for her to say more about it, but she didn't. She just patted the chair next to her and said, "Thomas, come have some breakfast."

Grandma Betsy looked like she wanted to say something, but instead she frowned more and wiped her hands on her apron and went back into the kitchen. Thomas sat down next to his mom. He started to ask her where everyone else was, but he noticed she wasn't looking at him. He followed her smile up to the side entrance of the dining room, where Uncle Joe had just walked in.

Uncle Joe came over and tapped the feather on top of the headdress. Thomas could feel it sway a little, like he was outside and there was a breeze. "Ready for Thanksgiving!" Uncle Joe said, sitting down next to his mom. "I like that."

Thomas couldn't believe it. "That's what the girl at Friendly's said," he almost shouted.

Uncle Joe dished out pancakes for the three of them. Thomas was surprised by how big his arms were. His dad's arms were skinny, like branches on a small tree, and very white; his Uncle Joe's were orangey, almost brown. "Well," Uncle Joe said, "Friendly's makes pretty good ice cream, so their waitresses probably know what they're talking about." Then he turned to Thomas's mom and said, "God, I haven't been there in years."

His mom didn't say anything. She kept smiling and tucked her hair behind her ear. Thomas wasn't sure he'd ever seen her do that before.

Thomas took a bite of the first pancake; Uncle Joe had given him three, which seemed like more than he could ever eat. They never ate like this in the morning, only cereal or toast and orange juice.

"Why are your arms so brown?" he asked.

"Because I live on the sun," Uncle Joe said, smiling at him.

That took Thomas by surprise. No one could live on the sun; it was way too hot. Everyone knew that.

"Uncle Joe lives in New Mexico, remember?" his mom said. "That's really far south of here. It gets pretty hot."

Thomas stopped eating. It almost sounded like his mom was about to give him an Awesome Lesson. That never happened. Maybe his dad had told her about New Mexico, so that she could do it when he wasn't there.

CHAPTER TWENTY-TWO

"Where's Dad?" he asked.

"Dad and Grandpa Victor went to get the turkey," his mom said. Then she smiled at Uncle Joe. Thomas wondered if she'd made a joke in there somewhere that he didn't get.

He wondered if she was going to say anything else about New Mexico, or if this was an especially short Awesome Lesson, or if that was all she knew about it. She must not have known very much, because the next thing she said was, "How did you sleep?"

"Not bad," his uncle said with a mouthful of pancakes, before Thomas could answer. "Though I must admit, it's a little strange to be back in the house and not sleeping in the room you and Paul are in. That was the room your dad and I shared when I was your age, Thomas." It took Thomas a moment to realize his mom hadn't been asking him how he'd slept; she'd been asking Uncle Joe. That seemed a little weird to him, but he was happy that he hadn't had to talk about it. It would kind of be a lie to say he just had an ordinary night.

His mom was nodding at Uncle Joe and smiling, still. She hadn't stopped. Thomas had thought he missed seeing her smile, but now he just thought she looked weird. When he came downstairs, he'd thought the smile was for him. He thought she'd know, somehow, that he'd seen her disappear, that he knew the secret now, that he was almost like a grown-up. But maybe it was stupid to think that she would know any of that without telling her. Carefully, he pulled off his headdress and placed it on the empty chair next to him.

"Hey, Mom," he said, but when she looked at him her face was the same, like she didn't notice anything different.

Grandma Betsy came out of the kitchen again. She was frowning, because there was no food in her hands. "All right," she said, handing Uncle Joe a piece of paper. "Here's the list."

She turned to Thomas and smiled, too wide. There was a little lipstick on one of her top teeth; you could hardly see it, but it was there. "Sweetheart, would you like to go into town with your uncle and help your grandma by getting some last-minute items?"

Uncle Joe gave him a thumbs-up. Thomas looked down at his plate; he'd eaten half of one pancake, and he was already full. He looked back up at his grandma and nodded. She came over to him and kissed his cheek, gripping each side of his face with her hands like if she didn't do that he might escape.

After she went back into the kitchen, Joe turned to his mom and said, "I suppose it's OK if you come along, too." His mom seemed to think that was the funniest thing anyone had ever said.

They must have renovated this town at some point, Annie thought. The sidewalks seemed a little wider, the exteriors of the antique shops cleaner. In place of nondescript hardware stores and aging beauty parlors, the town's main street was dotted with the tiny, sparse knick-knack shops that were ubiquitous in Carroll Gardens, which sold little bags and paperweights which were useless, but somehow worth exorbitant amounts of money. These things, the shops seemed to suggest, are the stuff of maturity and status. If they seem overpriced, then they aren't intended for you.

Then again, maybe the town seemed different because she was seeing it through different eyes. Mercifully, Joe did not stop at every rock and tree to describe the significant personal and historical events that had taken place there, and she did not have to indulge Awesome Lesson after Awesome Lesson about the history of New Hampshire, in which Tuftonboro had apparently played a vital and much-overlooked role. Mostly, Joe followed Thomas's lead, content to indulge the boy's curiosity about whatever struck him. Annie walked a little ways behind them, watched and smiled, and tried to keep away the thought that wouldn't go away: Now *this* is a good father.

Their destination was a wide-aisled high-end supermarket called Putnam's Family Grocery. The best word to describe this place, Annie thought, was *white*—it was a needless description in New Hampshire, especially given the sea of creperies and tchotchke stands they'd just passed on Tuftonboro's main street, but this supermarket seemed like where whiteness was born, and where it came to get whiter. She felt a twinge of pride at her own upbringing, and her insistence on not raising Thomas in a place like this. While Carroll Gardens was not exactly the picture of diversity, she could at least be certain that her son had seen people who didn't look like him on the subway, on the streets of Manhattan, at his school. It occurred to her that Paul had never mentioned the first time he met a black person, or anyone Hispanic or Asian or Jewish, for that matter. Surveying the pristine aisles of Putnam's, which the sign outside proclaimed had been serving Tuftonboro proudly since 1948, she realized it was entirely possible that it hadn't happened until college. The thought made her feel sorry for him, which she loved.

It wasn't an especially long excursion. Joe parked several blocks away from the supermarket, so that they'd be able to see the town as they walked there, but that only took half an hour. Once they reached their destination, Annie knew that she'd have to start counting the minutes before they were back with everyone else.

"Thomas," she said, crouching to his eye level. The position hurt her hips, but she'd noticed that he'd responded well when she spoke to him that way in the Friendly's parking lot. "Do you want to get some of the stuff on the list and meet us at the checkout line?"

Thomas gave her a look that was hard to take as anything but suspicion. She told herself that she was being paranoid; he just wasn't used to being told he could go off by himself.

"Don't worry," she said, casting a sideways look and a smile up at Joe, hoping she looked good from this angle, "we're in the safest town in the world."

Joe laughed and said, "Something like that." This seemed to satisfy Thomas, although he continued to look at her strangely as he took the half of the list that Joe handed him and headed off into the produce aisle.

It was only a matter of seconds before she couldn't even see him anymore, and she was standing alone with Joe. As soon as Thomas was gone, she felt her face grow hot; she had no idea how to explain sending him away.

Joe spoke before she could. "I suppose it's nice to have a little breathing room, huh?"

Annie laughed nervously, in spite of herself. Was he as eager to find a harmless excuse as she was? "Don't tell anyone," she said.

She remembered how easily flirting had come with Jack at the bar, after she'd worked through her initial fear. When she thought back to that night, she was impressed with how well she'd improvised some of those lines. The setting had helped, of course: the smell of layers of stale alcohol was as powerful a social lubricant as the absence of her son; that, and the fact that the man in question had been in no way related to her husband.

"What's first?" Joe asked. For a moment, she didn't know what he was referring to, and her imagination took over. Maybe this was going to be easier than she thought.

"Oh," she said, as he began to inspect the list, and, feeling that she should say something, added, "I don't know."

After a moment, he looked up from the list. "Buttermilk."

Something about the ridiculousness of that word at this particular moment, the very New Englandness of it, told her all she needed to know. He had no notion that anything off-color was happening. He was helping his mother complete her Thanksgiving meal, in the supermarket his family had been patronizing proudly since 1948.

Still, circumstances were on her side: for now, she had this shrunken-down version of reality, in which the two of them were alone, in safe, neutral territory. Safe—there weren't many places or people she could say that about anymore.

"So is this the supermarket your family came to when you were growing up?" she asked, then decided the question was asinine, and tried to recover with an even worse one. "What are supermarkets like in New Mexico?"

"Yes," he said, "and smaller." He looked towards the ceiling as he spoke, as if anything worth looking for on these shelves was high up. She wondered if the people they passed in the aisles thought they were a couple; why else would two adults be following a shopping list around? It was so blissfully mundane. She remembered reveling in trivial things like that when she and Paul were first married, how they'd made her feel so stupidly lucky.

"Tell me more about New Mexico," she said. She didn't like the way it came out—*tell me*—like he was a character from a fairytale. But that wasn't so far off, after all. There was something unreal about him, this gentler, simpler, more handsome version of her husband, especially the fact that three days earlier, she couldn't have imagined she'd be standing next to him now, with Paul nowhere in sight.

"It's beautiful," he said, navigating them away from the dairy aisle, towards the sugar and flour. "I didn't believe the hype before I got there, but now that I'm there, I think it's entirely deserved." Annie smiled and didn't say anything; she didn't want to admit that she didn't know what "the hype" was.

"I've never been," she offered. He couldn't fault her for that, hopefully.

"You haven't?" He stopped and turned to her. She touched her face absently, feeling the weight of his eyes. This was, she recognized, the first time he'd looked at her as anything besides a piece of scenery. It was a look that, if all were right with the world, he would have exchanged with her when they first bumped into each other in the doorway, mirroring her as she drank in something strange and exciting for the first time. "Well," he said, "then you'll have to come visit."

The supermarket was crowded, and seemed to be in constant flux. Annie hadn't noticed anyone stop long enough to take something down off a shelf and examine it since they got there. It was Thanksgiving, and everyone in the town was preparing a meal for more people than their kitchens and dining rooms could take, or was on their way somewhere, fretting about what to bring. Everyone here had forgotten something; they were all frantic, prematurely exhausted, not yet wearing their good clothes, not looking at anyone, hoping not to run into someone they knew and get pulled into a conversation. She and Joe were moving in slow motion, or maybe it only seemed that way, and now they'd stopped; the buzz of sound around them was caught by this moment, and the silence hanging between them, a space of only a few inches. It was her turn to speak.

"Yes," she said. "I'd like that."

As if she were a gas station attendant or a bank teller or an estranged sister-in-law, Joe smiled and nodded and went back to shopping. It was fine with her. She couldn't possibly have expected a moment like that to sustain itself for much longer. In that five-second world, Paul and Thomas and Joe's girlfriend Carly didn't exist.

Thomas was waiting for them at the checkout line, looking bored. Annie knelt down again—she was getting used to it. "Did you get everything?"

Thomas shrugged and showed her the list. Each item was preceded by a penciled-in, sloppily oversized check mark, pointing the wrong way. Annie was touched by the childishness of it. She wondered how long he'd been carrying a pencil around with him. "Good work," she said.

"May I?" Joe asked, dipping the basket to allow Thomas to put in his share.

She held Thomas's hand as she watched Joe pay and make small talk with the cashier. Pleasantries rolled off his skin like rain. Maybe it was the New England in him.

23

When Paul thought of his father, he heard his mother's voice saying, "Your father's had a long day." Victor had been a veterinarian in Mirror Lake, the town south of them. He often worked long hours and came home late in the evening to eat the solitary meal Betsy would fix specially for him, and it was understood that this meal was intended to remain solitary, with no interruptions. Now, he was retired, and Betsy took care of the bed and breakfast, but Paul still felt like he was interrupting his father from something important whenever he talked to him.

"You ready?" Paul asked. His father was washing his breakfast dish, so slowly that it was almost an art.

Victor nodded once and said, "I'll go warm up the car." The silent nod was his father's only form of affirmation. If he ever said the word "Yes," Paul might wonder if he was drunk.

Paul could remember two times—once in sixth grade, and again his junior year in high school—when his father had said, "Nice job," after he brought home his report card. Joe told him once that he had a similar vivid memory, of their father thumping him on the back, once, soundly, after a basketball game. Besides the reliable memory of him slumped over the dining room table, picking at whatever his mother had cooked for him with the kind of unflappable scrutiny Paul imagined he used for ailing cats and dogs, the image that stood out to him was of his father's impossibly tall frame, blocking out the light from the front hallway of the high school as he stood at the back of the auditorium to watch the orchestra's Christmas recital. Paul never knew whether he refused to sit in the seats because he was self-conscious about his height and afraid someone might ask him to move, or if he thought the idea of remaining seated for a high school orchestra concert was beneath him.

As Paul walked down the steps of the front porch to join Victor in the car, he felt the same brief, suspended panic he'd feel as a teenager, on rare nights when his mother had bridge club and Joe was at basketball practice: in a few moments, he would have to be alone with his father. He had to either think of something to talk about now, or sit in silence for forty minutes. Never mind that they hadn't seen each other in at least a year; to his father, sharing a car ride was as much catching up as two grown men could be expected to endure.

"We're going to the Brownings'," Victor said as he got into the car, "over in Ossipee."

Paul nodded immediately, as if the statement had been a test to see if he would approve. "Good," he said. "The Brownings'."

The landscape of Spring Tavern Road, which led west towards Arthur and Cecelia Browning's turkey farm, lent itself to quiet, especially this time of year. Unpeopled meadows along the road sparkled gray-green with morning frost and a low fog hung over the ground. The leaves were gone by now, everywhere—late September into early October was the season for spectacular leaves, and once November came it was hard to believe the bare monoliths dotting the landscape had ever been worth looking at. Theirs was the only car on the road, which stretched on for miles in every direction, like a highway through the desert.

Paul was so busy trying to think of an innocuous subject that would carry them to the farm and back that he almost didn't notice when his father spoke first. "How's the boy taking it?"

The car seemed colder than it had been a moment ago. Was this really happening—the moment when Victor revealed that he'd been paying more attention than Paul had given him credit for, that he could sense that things were bad between him and Annie? Maybe he'd even offer him some unprecedented fatherly advice—this would be the first time. "The attacks," Victor continued. "I imagine he's probably a bit shaken up."

Paul didn't know if he was relieved or disappointed. "Not anymore," he said. He remembered that whatever else he was, his father was one of those outside observers who'd been watching New York collapse and rebuild on television, wondering what the people there were thinking and doing, how they could possibly get up and live their lives every day. He tried to remember when that was reality for him, too, before everything else started to move in and fill his landscape. "Everyone was shaken up, I guess."

Victor shook his head, as if Paul had made an objective mistake. "But a kid," he said. "That would be a hard thing for a kid."

Paul agreed that it was very scary for Thomas, and for a lot of kids his age.

Victor sighed, as if he were trying to communicate with an idiot. "Well?"

Paul waited. His father said nothing. "Well what, Dad?"

"How is he? What are you doing about it?"

It was the most worked up he'd seen his father in years. Paul fought down the urge to laugh. Maybe all it took to get this man to show any concern for his family was a global-scale tragedy.

They'd reached the Brownings' farm, where a fat ruddy man wearing a plaid hunter's hat with earflaps was trotting towards his car on the other side of the lot, clutching a bag that bulged with the carcass of a turkey as big as him. Victor let the car idle and didn't move. Paul knew he was waiting for an answer.

"He's seeing a therapist in Manhattan," Paul said, looking at his lap. "He's been very helpful."

Victor nodded. "Glad to hear it," he said. "I'll be back in a minute. Pop the trunk."

His father opened the car door and walked out into the cold, no jacket, hunched over, hands thrust deep into his pants pockets, practically skipping to keep warm.

The ride back was silent, and Paul was glad to have it that way. He clenched and unclenched his fist and watched his breath dance like smoke in front of his face. *This piece of shit Ford Escort*, he thought. *Warm up the car, my balls.*

"Quit that," his father snapped at one point, out of nowhere. "A few years in New York and you can't sit still." Without realizing it, he'd been drumming his fingers on the windowsill. They retreated slowly into his palm, as if their feelings were hurt, as he repeated the words in his mind. *Can't sit still?* Is that what his father thought of

New York; that, and the part about terrorism? His parents hadn't visited him there since his graduation from Columbia, despite several promises and what felt like thousands of times Paul and his family had trekked up to New Hampshire. He wondered if they'd ever visited his brother in New Mexico, and almost asked.

It's just as well that he doesn't have any idea about what's really going on, he thought, as Victor heaved an old-man, brink-of-death wheeze, loaded with phlegm and a finely-aged will to ignore physical ailments. Why should this man know any more about his marital troubles than anyone else—literally, anyone else in the world, besides him and Annie and possibly Scheckman the Great, whose insights meant precisely fuck-all at this point?

If anyone should be privy to the intimate workings of his marriage, it was Kathy Burke. If it was going to happen, sooner or later—Paul imagined theirs as an inevitable affair, two people whose erotic fates were innately intertwined by forces beyond their control—it seemed as natural a cause as any that she would offer to be his shoulder to cry on. She would pop in for one of her no longer uncommon impromptu visits, and he wouldn't be able to contain himself: he was sorry for making such a scene in front of her, but to tell her the absolute truth, things were not good, Kathy, not good at all. He and Annie simply weren't working anymore, and he'd been harboring deep, undeniable feelings for someone at work—

"Shit," his father said. "Defroster's acting up again."

But of all things, September 11th? That was the best Victor could do? For the first time in his life, the hulking refrigerator he called his father had come close to recognizing him not simply as a fellow human being, and the most concern he could muster up was parroting every pundit and crybaby on national television?

"Thomas?" he should have said. "You mean my son? He's afraid of his pet turtle, but he also seems to like it more than he likes me. I have no fucking idea what scares him. I don't know anything about him. Like father like son, huh Pop?"

He should have told his father that in the middle of the night, when he awoke to the sounds of his child screaming in the next room, he was *relieved* to find him that way, because at least that meant he hadn't been murdered in his bed by his own mother. That those images Victor thought were straight out of a mental patient's nightmare, the double inferno of the planes hitting the towers and the relentless visions of being on one of those planes, in one of those towers, whatever plagued him when he closed his eyes, it all seemed like nothing. Make-believe.

"September 11th," he should have said, "was an enormous inconvenience. It was practically impossible to get downtown. The Manhattan Bridge exit was closed for months." And in retrospect, with everything that had happened since, it would have been the truth.

After they pulled into the driveway, his father exited the car with a savage quickness that kept his face entirely hidden. Paul knew they wouldn't talk again for the rest of the visit.

Victor walked up the driveway to the house, cradling the turkey like a sick child. For a moment, Paul imagined his father's thin arms bowing out like branches, unable to bear the dead animal weight. He imagined the soft thud as it hit the snow, like a gunshot in the distance. He imagined his father staring down at the thing, face-to-face with his failure to provide for his family on the day when the entire country expected nothing less. He would look to his son, and the crow's feet around his eyes would open up, his unusually dark brown eyes pleading for a solution, and Paul would have none, and offer none. He'd shrug his shoulders and walk past his father into the house.

Instead, Victor pushed forward as if he was carrying a pillow, the crunch of his boots in the snow keeping the same rhythm as when there was no extra weight. His father didn't ask him to get the door for him, or grab anything from the car. He didn't need his help.

The cold air worked its way into Paul's warm clothes, permeating each layer until it found his skin and stayed there, but he stayed where he was, standing next to the Ford. His own car was in the driveway, a few feet away. He didn't know where his wife and son were. For a moment, all he could think of was driving away.

He recognized the slow muted crescendo behind him: the sound of tires on snow, which used to mean that his father was home from work on winter evenings. A gentle honk startled him, and he backed away, feeling conspicuously empty-handed. Behind the wheel, his brother was smiling, but Annie was giving him a strange look. He couldn't see Thomas's face, but knew he was there because of the unnaturally dyed orange and blue feathers touching the ceiling in the back seat.

Thomas came out with two plastic bags and handed one to Joe. "Thanks, Buddy," his brother said, then rubbed Thomas's head—a little too roughly, Paul thought.

Joe wasn't wearing a jacket. Some things never changed. The sight of his arms was like a calling card in the halls of their high school. Sometimes a girl Paul had never talked to before would come up to him in the hall and say something like, "I know you—your brother's the guy who doesn't wear a jacket, right?" For a brief moment, he'd had the idea to emulate his little brother, but he hated being cold—he was so skinny the air went right through to his bones. Besides, he knew that his mother wouldn't let him anywhere near the door in only shirt-sleeves, since as a child he'd spent most winters bedridden like some kind of Victorian invalid.

That Joe had kept up the habit for twenty-five years didn't surprise Paul at all. He recognized the curious, half-hypnotized expression on Annie's face as she watched him unloading groceries from the trunk. Each of Joe's successive girlfriends had had a similar look as they watched him playing basketball or jumping off their dock into the lake. Now, apparently, he was doing some kind of generic manual labor, tossing pieces of metal around in the sun, and he was sure that sometimes the yoga instructor or whoever she was would bring him his lunch and watch with the same expression.

And still, Paul was certain, his brother did everything with infuriating ease, as if anyone who wasn't doing exactly what he was, who didn't have a sense of monastic calm and a winning smile and a yoga instructor waiting in bed for him, was simply missing some fundamental fact about life, that all one needed to do was relax and everything meaningful would simply throw itself at him. Joe was a man who would die happy. At a certain point, Paul had realized he couldn't bear to be around it anymore.

As they walked away from him towards the house, Joe said something Paul couldn't hear and Annie laughed. Thomas stayed with him. "We got groceries," he said, throwing his neck back to look up at Paul, as if he was taller than he actually was. "For Grandma."

"Uh-huh." He took Thomas's hand and walked to the house with him. "What did you think of the town? Did it live up to the Awesome Lessons?"

Thomas shrugged. Paul felt too tired to bother going any further with his line of questioning, or to be offended. He stopped at the front porch and kneeled down in front of his son. "You doing OK today—" he stopped himself, realizing he was about to call him "Buddy," which he hated, "—old pal?" Thomas nodded. He didn't ask what Paul meant.

"I'm OK," Thomas said. He looked off towards the lake, then rubbed his hands on his arms. Paul noticed no one had made him wear gloves. "Mom says it's always hot where Uncle Joe lives. Is that true?"

He could hear the tinkering of dinner preparations inside. He'd crossed the threshold; he was closer to the house now than he was to the car. Still, he could grab Thomas by the hand and make a run for it. This could be a do over for his mistake in France. This time, he could leave with what mattered.

Paul heard his mother's voice asking about the whereabouts of her "boys." Joe said something else that made his wife laugh. For a moment, he entertained the thought that if he and Thomas left now, they might not even be missed.

"Mom said that?" he asked. Thomas nodded.

Paul stood up and began to walk inside. He stopped in the hallway, where he could still turn around before it was too late. He caught a quick glimpse of his father through the doorway, in the kitchen. They made eye contact for less than a second. "Good thing it's Thanksgiving," he said to Thomas, as they walked into the kitchen together. "I'm so hungry I could eat two turkeys."

24

His smirk was a tangible presence in the room. "Paul," she said, "if you've got something to say to me, just say it. I'm trying to sleep."

"Aren't we all," he said, then laughed to himself. The mark of a truly small man, she thought; laughing at his own jokes.

"I just find the situation funny, that's all."

"What situation?"

He propped himself up on his elbow, a gesture which felt too intimate. "Here I am," he said, "in the house where I spent my formative years, after going out in the world and beginning my own independent life, and it turns out that nothing's changed from when I lived here twenty-five years ago."

Annie spread out her arms on either side of her. This sounded suspiciously far from an attack on her. "I don't know what you mean," she said.

Paul breathed a sad version of laughter. "My brother," he said. "He still wins everyone over."

She made a conscious effort to remain very still. Several possible responses floated to the surface, then dissipated.

"I think," Paul went on, "there are some things we're not meant to ever understand. We can grow and mature in all directions, but some things that are fundamentally close to us are supposed to remain mysteries until we die. For me, it's my brother."

Annie debated saying something, and settled on silence again.

"I don't see it," he continued. "The charm or the wit or the brilliance or the... I don't know, *magnetism*, I guess. The ability to make bullshit sound like success."

The sudden hostility ignited something familiar in her. She responded without thinking. "What does that mean?"

Paul turned and looked at her. It was scary: in so many ways, they had no business sharing a bed, but there it was, the undeniable truth of their proximity, and of its permanence. *This isn't going to change unless someone changes it.* The thought was so clear and so sudden she was afraid she'd said it out loud.

"I'm only telling you this because you're the only one here to talk to," he said. "I don't expect you to understand. You were under his spell, too, obviously." He turned away to lay on his back and clasped his hands together on his chest. "I don't know whether I expected better of you or not," he said to the ceiling.

She willed herself to ignore him. She'd had to endure his family's backwards version of Thanksgiving, their backwards version of family, and she didn't have to take any more, not tonight.

When she was growing up, her parents always hosted Thanksgiving, squeezing the entire extended family into their modestly-sized apartment on 92nd Street. Not all the food could fit on the table, so everyone went back and forth to the kitchen to serve themselves; at no point was everyone seated together at the table. Children sat on the living room floor, in front of the television, where the Macy's Parade provided a tinny soundtrack to the four or five lively conversations which were going on simultaneously. There was always at least one argument, a heated political debate or something more personal, and by the time the pies were brought out it didn't matter anymore. There was a perfect rhythm to it, a bumpy predictability that made Annie overly sentimental about things like the smell of pumpkin pie and a knife gliding through a gelatinized cylinder of canned cranberry sauce.

Betsy's table was set ahead of time. She remained seated for the entire meal, not once remembering something she'd left in the kitchen. The food was gratingly pleasant—not a seasoning out of place. Annie could taste years of practice in the green beans amandine and sweet potato casserole. There was nothing surprising for Betsy, no new ideas or experiments, and God knows how long it had been that way.

The Mayfield Thanksgiving was a symphony of clinks and creaks. Each time someone spoke, it was like the first line in a play: the sound of a human voice would have to cut through layers of cold and quiet, and their words would linger, ready to shatter, until someone else took up the challenge and responded.

All of it was bearable to her this year—blissfully, hilariously bearable. Joe sat across from her. She was uninhibited about looking up and smiling whenever the desire struck her, which was often. In the silence, there was plenty of space for her to create her own rhythm: look down, chew, look up, wait for eye contact, smile. She imagined him creating a similar rhythm, and cherished the moments when they synced up and looked at each other at the same time. Rather than focusing on the potentially stifling tension of right now, she imagined a month or two from now, going over this moment with him and laughing about it. She took in every piece of him that she could see—neck, right arm, left arm, hair, cheeks, chin, mouth—and thought of the parts beneath the table, all of it, being hers, a lover's entitlement.

She'd drafted a mental postcard: *Albuquerque is warm this time of year. It's always warm, really. But right now it's spectacular. Is it raining in New York? There's a part of the late fall where it seems to rain every day. Thomas loves his new school and is doing well. To answer your question, Paul, no, we won't be coming back. Don't get too wet.*

Now, she rolled over in bed, where she could hide whatever facial expression might occur as she thought about his brother. "I don't know what you're talking about, Paul. It seems to me that you're overly critical of Joe. I don't see what I have to do with it."

An uneven vibration disturbed the sheets. It was him laughing, again. "All right," he said, "have it your way. I still say you were acting like a smitten little girl."

She closed her eyes. She wasn't tired and she didn't care. She'd wander up and down the halls of this whole house and out into the night, and she'd still feel rested. If she wanted to, she could leave the bed and fly.

The room was quiet, the last words fading out of her memory. She felt a loosening in her and was slipping towards sleep when Paul threw his final two cents into the dark room. "It doesn't matter, Annie. Really, it doesn't matter to me at all."

25

They'd just gotten there, and now they were leaving. Vacations were stupid. Everyone looked forward to them like they were special, but really, it was just a few days, and then you were back at school, back home in your own room.

Thomas really didn't want to leave. He stood on the porch and argued with his dad. He said stuff like, "I haven't missed school all year." His dad looked tired. Thomas knew he shouldn't be making a scene in front of his grandparents, and he knew he should have thrown the headdress out by now, but he couldn't help it. Something about the old scary house had given him powers, and when they got back to Brooklyn, he was sure he wouldn't be able to do it anymore, and in Brooklyn was where he really needed it.

Grandma Betsy was on the other side of his dad, smiling at him and holding her chest with one hand as if her insides were about to pop out. Thomas felt bad; he didn't want his grandma to think that he wanted to stay because of her, since that wasn't the truth. For a moment Thomas thought of asking her if she wanted to trade places with him for a while and take care of Alexander in Brooklyn, but then he realized that that meant he'd have to be all alone in the house with Grandpa Victor.

His grandpa was loading up the car for them. Each time he took a bag, he bent down the way his gym teacher had said was bad for your back, like he was trying to touch his toes. He'd spent a lot of time in the past few days coming up behind Thomas and holding onto his shoulder, tight. Too tight. It was like he was giving him something. Thomas had one theory that his grandpa was the one who'd given him the ability to see people disappearing. You could tell just by looking at him that he had done some monstering in his life; he was probably an expert at it. Thomas even wondered if, in his old age, his grandpa was losing his ability to change back, because when you looked at him quickly sometimes it was hard to tell.

At the other end of the long porch, his mom was saying goodbye to his uncle Joe. There was a line where the sun started and the shadows stopped, and Mom and Uncle Joe were standing in the light part, facing each other. Uncle Joe had his hands in his pockets and his mother had her hands behind her back. They looked like something Thomas had seen in a movie once. His mother looked happy again, the way she had when they'd all gone shopping. Besides seeing her disappear, that had been his favorite part of the whole vacation. He wanted to join them, but he wanted to keep trying to convince his dad to let them stay longer. Besides, it didn't look like there was quite enough room for him over there; the sun was feeding the floor in the space between their bodies, and if he stood there he'd be blocking it out.

Grandpa Victor closed the trunk. It was the loudest noise Thomas had ever heard. Everything was loud in the snow. He saw his grandpa slap his hands together, like, *Well, all done.* Thomas took his dad's hand and tried again.

"It's safer here," he said. "New York isn't safe anymore. That's what everybody says. Leave me here and I'll be safe."

For some reason, right after he said that, his dad looked up at Grandpa Victor, who raised his eyebrows back at him. His face was long, like an old mirror. "I am not leaving you here," his father said.

Thomas felt a hand on his back and somehow he knew it was his mother's. "We have to go back," she said, and before he knew what was happening, she reached up with her other hand and pulled off his headdress.

She'd take Thomas with her. They'd pick a good school for him, maybe some private place that believed in art instead of grades and taught classes in adobe huts. Maybe they'd live in an adobe hut. Maybe she'd finally learn Spanish; Joe would give her lessons in the bathtub.

If only there were some way to get out of the house tonight, once they got back. The thought of coming back from this only to retire to the silence of Henry Street, playing guessing games about whether or not the person next to her was really sleeping, was like putting everything that had happened in a bottle and shoving it on a bottom shelf. She wanted to go out; she wanted to hop out of the car in midtown and find Jack from the bar. She'd get really drunk this time, and she'd tell him everything, and if he tried to stop things she'd make him keep going. None of it mattered. She felt like she'd just given her two weeks' notice at a job she hated, and now she was going to come in late every day and take two hours for lunch.

This was usually her favorite sight, the enormous house shrinking behind them in the distance as they drove south towards civilization, but Joe's flight wasn't until the next day so he was there too, sliding away back into estrangement, growing smaller and smaller until she couldn't read the expression on his face anymore. She let his parting words burn close to her—"Have a safe trip home," he'd said.

"Hey! What are you doing?"

She glanced at the back seat, irritated. The sudden yelp had startled her, and, worse, shoved Joe's features into a half-dissolved mess. "What is it, Thomas?"

"What are you doing?" he said again, lurching his small body forward into the front seat.

"Hey, sit back," Paul said, swatting behind him.

Thomas didn't move. "That's mine! You're ruining it!"

Annie looked down at the thing in her lap. There was a sloppy dried-glue mark where she'd absently twisted one of the feathers off. "Sorry, sweetie," she said. "It was coming apart anyway."

"Give it to me," he said. Annie handed him the sorry remains of his headdress, which he promptly yanked onto his head.

She smiled at him in the rearview mirror. "You look like King of the Art Supply Closet," she said. Thomas scowled. He really was a cute kid.

Paul shook his head. "Jesus," he muttered. Annie didn't bother to ask him what he meant by it, or try to figure it out. She was past that now.

She leaned her seat back and turned to look out the window. "Just shut up, Paul," she whispered, closing her eyes. "Just shut the fuck up."

He would not put her in charge of finding a person for Thomas to see. *Person*—he didn't even know the right name for it, for a kid his age. Therapist? Specialist? Shrink? Everything made it sound like he'd be investigated, poked at like a bad piece of fruit.

He loved him so much. It was one of those facts so simple that it had to renew itself constantly to make any sense. He loved his son. He was worried about him. He was afraid.

He didn't want Annie anymore, and he didn't need her—if he woke up tomorrow and she wasn't there, it would be like someone had handed him a new, better life. He looked at Thomas in the back seat, biting back tears after what his own mother had done to the object he seemed to care about so much. He was damaged, certainly, but he would be OK. He just needed some help, and then he'd be OK.

"Hey, old pal," he said, overly cheerful, looking into the rearview mirror as he spoke. "Still looks pretty good. I was thinking maybe we could get another one of those ice cream guys later, what do you say?"

Thomas just shrugged. He didn't seem to be putting it on, either, unlike his mother, who was feigning sleep like a pro in the seat next to him, an infuriating little smile haunting her lips.

Fine, he thought. This is fine. She can stay, but I'm in charge. I'll do whatever it is that needs to be done.

PART III

Rough Guide

26

Most kids didn't want to go outside when it was cold, but the lunch monitors were old and nice and let people go outside if they wanted to, anyway. Ingrid looked like a cupcake all bundled up in pink and purple and yellow. Thomas couldn't tell where her coat ended and her scarf began. A few pieces of hair escaped from under her hat, which was yellow with little pink strawberries all over it. Her face was red and her skin was shiny above her lip from snot. Thomas didn't think anyone else could look pretty with snot coming out of their nose.

They were at the swings again, but they weren't swinging. The chains creaked, making haunted house noises as they pushed back and forth in the frozen dirt with their toes.

"So," she said, "you talked to her, but she didn't hear you? But she was there, in your room?"

Thomas nodded proudly. Ingrid seemed impressed, which almost never happened.

"Were you having a dream?"

"Nope." He thought about telling Ingrid about his dream, but decided not to. He still hadn't told his mom yet, and he thought she should be the first to know. He'd promised her, after all. "I wasn't dreaming anything."

"Wow," said Ingrid. Thomas waited for her to say something else, but she didn't. Instead, he asked her about her two Thanksgivings.

"Oh, oh, oh, guess what!" she said, louder than she usually spoke, bouncing up and down in the swing. "My parents are getting back together!"

She looked like she was waiting for him to say something, so he said, "What about Fraidy?"

Ingrid frowned. "What about Fraidy? What do you mean?"

"Do you get to keep her?"

She shook her head and rolled her eyes. That was the opposite of saying *Wow* and looking impressed. That happened even less often. "Why wouldn't I get to keep her, Thomas?"

"Because—" Thomas could feel his nose running now, and he wiped it with the back of his mitten. He probably looked like a baby. "Because you got her because your parents were fighting."

She rolled her eyes again. It was really getting cold now. "That's not how it works," she said.

Why were they even out here? When it got cold, the lunch monitors cleared off the tables in the cafeteria and you could play Uno or Guess Who. Thomas didn't know when Ingrid had decided she was too good to sit inside and play Guess Who with him, or why she thought it was cooler to be outside in the stupid freezing cold. And what did that even mean, her parents were getting back together? That wasn't a real thing, was it?

"Well," said Thomas, "my mom's in love."

Ingrid smiled. She looked kind of mean. "Really?" she said. "How do you know?"

"Because I know," said Thomas. "I was there when it happened. She met someone really great, better than my dad, and they're in love."

Ingrid looked like she was about to roll her eyes again, but didn't. "Who is he?"

Thomas bit his lip. Something told him Ingrid wouldn't like the real answer if he told her. "She met him in New Hampshire," he said. "His name is Joe, and he lives in New Mexico."

Ingrid nodded, thinking it over. "Is *he* in love with *her*?" she asked.

Thomas had no idea. He hadn't even thought of that. He wasn't even sure about his mother, really; he'd just wanted to say something. "Yes," he said. "He is. I bet they're going to get married, too."

Ingrid was quiet for a while after that. She dragged the toe of her boot on the sparkling frosty ground and twisted the swing back and forth. He felt a little bad for not letting her say more about her parents, but she had been mean when he'd asked her about Fraidy, and he was still pretty sure "getting back together" didn't really exist, so really there was no point. "Well, that's great," she said finally, "for your mom."

The bell rang. There had only been two other kids on the playground with them, by the jungle gym, and they'd gone in already. It was just the two of them now, with the old lunch monitor walking towards them and saying something. She looked tiny, like she was a thousand miles away. It reminded him of how quiet everything was at his grandparents' house, where all you could see was snow and you couldn't hear anything but sudden loud noises, like the car door. He wanted to tell Ingrid about it, but then he decided not to.

27

In the past, finals season was the time of year when Paul was most excited to get home from work. It brought out the worst in his students—he might as well be working at a prestigious research university, the way they clawed at every possibility for an extra point or two for their GPA. Kids who hadn't spoken all semester were suddenly the worst offenders, turning up at his office with scowls, begging for extensions or defending their painfully incorrect answers. It brought out the worst in him, too. "This isn't high school," he'd say to their backs as they stormed out to tell whoever was waiting outside, *Good luck, this asshole's not going to budge.*

At home, Annie would listen. She'd make him feel like if he could do it over again with her there, he'd think of something nicer to say. "I'm one of those teachers you can tell doesn't want to be there. Just a failed chemist shoved into a college gig," he'd told her once, as she stroked his hair in her lap. "I can't think of anything more pathetic."

Up there, she'd looked pretty and far away, like someone else's wife that he was borrowing for an evening.

She'd say something generically soothing, or just stay quiet, and he'd feel better. Not like the problem was solved, but still better, like life was inevitable and everyone's problems made sense.

Even on less rough days, he'd been eager to get home, which seemed so quiet and sane compared to the college. The lights were softer, and he knew the two other people who would be there. It was simple, but true, and it made the hours between six and seven seem to slip by faster, and the commute through Crown Heights and Park Slope blur, until Henry Street came into focus.

It helped that it was December. Paul had an uncharacteristic soft spot for Christmastime, and an even less characteristic preference for Christmas in New York over New England. What was lacking in predictable annual desserts and door-to-door carolers was made up for by an entire metropolis on its best behavior, dropping its pretense of superiority for innocent, outdated decorations and glitter everywhere. Thomas's upbringing had been entirely secular, but they had instilled in him a love of American Christmas nonetheless. Paul wasn't sure if he'd picked up the Nativity story somewhere along the way, but he knew that his son was well-versed in *Miracle on 34th Street* and ice skating at Rockefeller Center.

In what Paul found to be a particularly low blow to the nation's intelligence, for the past year the media had been trying to spin gross consumerism as patriotism. He was urged, even more so than usual, to go out and buy everything he could, because otherwise, he was supposed to think, another three thousand people might die. The festive atmosphere that usually felt good-natured now felt desperate and lonely. "We'll be fine," everyone seemed to be saying, but no one really believed it.

This year, home was just a continuation of work. It was quieter, certainly, but it was not peaceful. Not refuge. Annie was somewhere else. Mondays and Wednesdays, as usual, were a lost cause, and when she was there, she was eerily happy, for reasons he knew had nothing to do with him. She'd been acting suspicious lately, humming to herself and wearing clothes he hadn't seen in years. He had several theories about what was going on, but at the end of the day, he didn't want to know. He just wanted her to be there for Thomas, and he was too exhausted to insist that *being there* mean anything more than literally being physically present, from time to time.

He had to stay late most nights to deal with the mess of the end of the semester. He'd take unnecessary bathroom breaks three or four times a night in the adolescent hope of running into Kathy, who'd stopped visiting as often. He tried to tell himself that she had exams to deal with, too, but the thought that won out was that she no longer found him more interesting than work. One evening, when his office was unusually free of whiny students and the quiet felt eerie, he decided to pay her a visit.

It was the first time he'd been in her office. Tortuously, it rose to the standards of his imagination: a dark, romantic fortress of academia. She was working by the light of an elegant, old-looking lamp. Her face was lit by a mixture of the blue light from the computer screen, which she leaned into with the intensity of someone trying to break a code, and the warm brown-orange from the lamp. She was out of place, a relic pounding away at technology beyond her time. It was adorable. Paul was sure she had no idea how archaic she looked, and that she didn't dress the way she did for effect. He couldn't imagine that Annie awoke a day in her life and went to her closet without a specific image in mind. How had he put up with it for so long?

"Knock knock," he said, and instantly felt stupid for saying it.

She seemed pleased enough to see him. Her startled eyes were priceless, huge and swimming behind the clunky glasses, her mousey face almost obscured by the vast nest of frizzy hair. "Hi, Paul," she said. "What can I do for you?"

She hadn't invited him to sit down, so he stood in the doorway. He longed to come in closer, but was afraid it might be seen as overstepping his bounds, literally. "I just thought—"

"Come in, come in!" she said, standing halfway up to clear a stack of papers off her desk.

He sat down in what he and his colleagues referred to as the Godfather seat, where students who chose to brave office hours stared up at their professor, flanked by a lifetime of books and diplomas, and felt that they were bargaining for their lives. Paul allowed his body to settle in, taking her invitation as a tremendously good sign. She folded her hands on the desk and smiled beneficently. He had her full attention.

"I just thought I might provide a little human contact," he said. "It can be hard to come by this time of year."

"Tell me about it," she said, sweeping her hand in a gesture indicating the piles of paper. Paul thought the phrase was beneath her, but he let it go.

"Those four walls can get pretty oppressive," he went on, moving his head back to indicate his office down the hall. Kathy nodded, saying nothing, and raised her eyebrows slightly, as if awaiting more.

He had no more. He hadn't come in with a plan, which in retrospect seemed like a horrible way to go about this. "Winter is tough," he said. "This college takes on a different character, you know? It's quiet and busy at the same time—God, what a deadly combination—and home isn't much better."

Kathy shifted in her chair. He went on.

"My wife isn't exactly a support these days," he said, and exhaled a brief, angry laugh. "We're not exactly a postcard of holiday cheer."

"Oh," she said, and reached across the Godfather desk to touch his hand. "Paul, I'm sorry."

He looked up at her, jolted by the contact. Was this happening? Had he fallen asleep at his desk grading papers and dreamed himself into this?

He turned his hand over so that he was grasping hers, fingers and all. It was a little bit of a stretch, but it was OK. She had made the first move. She had told him it was OK. It was time to do this. He began to talk.

"I think anyone can live with a sexless marriage, you know, even a *loveless* marriage—people do it all the time, from what I understand," he said. Something may have changed in her expression, but he ignored it and kept going. "And who am I to think I'm any better than those other people, who spend decades settling, making do with what they have? It's not like I'm destined for greatness; I have no such delusions. It's just that we have a *kid*, you know, and the kid sees the way we look at each other and I'm beginning to be genuinely afraid that our kid is *fucked*, that he's going to be some sick story you read about in a newspaper and you're glad it didn't happen to you, only it's really happening to me, and almost all of it I can handle but I can't handle that, and I just need—yes, I think I *do* need sex, Kathy, and, well, some love, because it's gotten to that point. Kathy." He leaned towards her. "The point is, would you have dinner with me?"

She adjusted her glasses. Her face looked nothing like it did in any of his fantasies. She looked frightened, sweaty, even a little stupid. She extricated her hand from his; her tiny, limp hand. "Paul," she said, "I'm sorry to hear about what you're going through, but—" He could tell she had no intention of finishing the sentence.

For the first time, he saw her sloppiness not as a masterfully sexy life decision, but for what it really was: a woman who'd never bothered to learn how to dress right, whose lack of style was an act of stubbornness. The only person more pathetic than this specimen was the person whose own life was so devoid of hope that he'd managed to make her into something desirable. It was like waking up after a year-long dream, finally remembering where he was.

He stood up before he spoke. "I'm sorry," he said, backing towards the door.

"Paul." She stood up too. "It's OK. I'm not—I don't want you to think that you did anything wrong—"

"I did." His hand flailed behind him for the doorknob.

"No, Paul, really. Look, I'm just swamped with finals at the moment. I really am sorry to hear about your family and if you need to talk, maybe after winter break—"

"It's OK." He opened the door and spoke mainly to the hallway. "Kathy, it's OK. Just—" He turned the knob back and forth in his hand, "—forget I said anything. Or don't. OK. Good night."

Back in his office, he packed up his things in a frenzy, as if there were an armed gunman roaming the halls. At some point he realized he was out of breath. The space in his mind which would normally be occupied by a vision of Kathy coming back to find him, knocking gingerly and slinking her way in, was emptied out, with only some unsavory residue left.

It was six thirty. He wanted a drink, but he didn't really drink. He wanted to leave, but he didn't know where he would go. *Winter break.*

It hadn't even occurred to him. They had no plan. There was nothing ahead but home.

There was nowhere else to go.

After they came back from New England, Mondays and Wednesdays stopped being fun, with one exception. Six days after Thanksgiving, she walked nine blocks south from the store to Union Square, fought her way through the Christmas crafts fair shoppers, and shook off her rainy coat sleeves in the foyer of their rival Pages, the one they referred to as The Beast, which towered over the farmer's market, the amateur skateboarders, the homeless scattered around the interior of the park, the well-groomed NYU kids and their shabbier New School counterparts, the midtown well-dressed, the hipsters passing through on their way to the L train, the Gramercy families, and the few who congregated at Pages, NPR loyals who ignored the store's corporate allegiances because of its stature and its history, who shunned her branch in favor of this one because of the universal feeling of envy you felt when you snuck into the children's section to use the bathroom on your way somewhere else and glimpsed, on your way up the escalator, people stretched for what seemed like miles in the sprawling Coffee Corner overlooking the park, or in the empty chairs of the event room, just reading, and you imagined they'd been like that for hours, having found one of those precious places in New York where one could stay warm, not pay, and not be bothered.

She found the travel section, picked up the first Albuquerque guidebook she saw—who could tell the difference between them?—and found a spot in some forgotten section on the fourth floor, on the windowsill, which may or may not have been intended as a seat. She found herself unable to read any page from beginning to end. Her attention was pulled away by each photo of an annual street fair or sidebar about an often-overlooked monument. This was a *good* guidebook, she decided; it was doing its job. By the time she'd scattered her gaze across every page, she felt that if she spent one more day away from this place she might die.

She felt something healthy radiating from just the orange light of the photographs; the pages seemed to glow. Albuquerque was all sand and sky and sun, each borrowing from the other, keeping each other warm.

New York was *frigid*. How had she overlooked this? What, exactly, was the upside of winds that could only be described as cruel, on top of sub-zero misery, and the occasional snow that stayed picturesque for one day before becoming brown mush? Who came up with the theory that tall buildings blocked out weather? Some idiot from the country with that provincial smugness that bred phrases like "a simpler way of life."

She bought the book and walked to Sixth Avenue to take the F train. It was only eight. She realized she hadn't eaten. It was at least three hours earlier than she usually came home. *Paul might suspect something*, she thought. Then, just as quickly: *It doesn't matter.* Nothing mattered—this had been her mantra since Thanksgiving, and she meant it.

She ordered take-out from the Thai place on Smith and Bergen, then went home. The house was empty, so she sat in the kitchen and ate out of the carton. She couldn't remember the last time she'd done this—it was so deliciously sloppy, so pure. It felt good to indulge a basic need in such a basic way. She didn't worry about where everyone was, just poked at the fat noodles with a plastic fork and let some of the brown, sticky sauce drip down her chin.

When she heard footsteps from upstairs, too heavy for a child, she allowed herself a moment of disappointment, then returned to the pleasure of the noodles. There seemed to be a long time between when she initially heard him upstairs and when he appeared in the doorway of the kitchen. Those forty seconds or so were some of the best of her entire year: the house was silent, as usual, but in that rare way she used to long for, when all the traffic and noise of the city seemed to pause so that she could enjoy her dinner. The room seemed to hum around her—it was her place. Paul was somewhere, but for now, he wasn't here, and she was a woman eating noodles in her own kitchen.

She let him stand there for a while before she chose to look up at him. *Maybe he'll notice*, she thought, *how content I am. Maybe some humanity will come between us, and he'll decide that whatever he has to say can wait a few more minutes.*

Instead, when she did acknowledge that he was there, the silent message that greeted her was unmistakable: *You are pathetic.* Like he'd come downstairs hoping to see anyone else, anything else, and had found her instead.

She turned back to her food, wiping some sauce off her lip. There were a few noodles left in scattered corners of the carton. She closed the lid and looked down at it.

"You're home early tonight," he said.

She shrugged. "Dr. Scheckman was—"

"Don't bother." It was a command, short and authoritative. He walked past her to the refrigerator, opened it and just stood there, like he'd forgotten what he wanted. It looked like he was showing her its contents, and waiting for her to say, "That's very nice," so that he could close the door.

"He was sick," she said weakly, to the table.

He closed the refrigerator and sat down across from her. "Why would you go to the trouble to make an imaginary person sick?"

"He's not imaginary," she said automatically. It was the response she'd had prepared since the beginning. *Go look him up if you want to,* was the next part. *Check the Internet. Check the Yellow Pages.* But it didn't seem worth it.

Paul shook his head. "Please don't do this anymore, OK? Just stop lying now."

She stared at the noodle remains. "How do you know? I mean, how did you find out?"

He didn't answer. She never did find out how he'd figured it out, or if he'd ever believed her in the first place.

"What do you do on Mondays and Wednesdays?" he asked, then slapped the table lazily and added, "No, don't tell me. I don't want to know."

"Paul."

She thought of telling him about the dream she had in France, that a woman she didn't recognize, with the same body and hair as her but blurry eyes and no mouth, tried to take Thomas away. The woman didn't say anything, but Annie understood that she was trying to tell her that she, not Annie, could keep him safe. Paul was there, but he didn't say anything. He almost let it happen. She couldn't see the knife in the dream, or feel it, but all of a sudden she became aware that she was dreaming, and she told the woman if she didn't let go of her son and leave forever, something horrible was going to happen, something unimaginable.

"I was with someone else," she said to Paul, staring down at her remaining noodles. "Another man, I mean." She'd imagined saying it many times; she'd had a strategy, a when and how. He'd be riding high on a wave of condescension, and then she'd slap him in the face, knock him out of orbit. In her fantasies, she laughed after she said it, her hands on her hips and her head thrown back.

It didn't happen that way. Her voice was unsure, adolescent; her words seemed to be trying to go back to where they came from.

"Once," she added. "Only once. And nothing really—"

"I was with someone else, too."

She heard herself gasp. He was winning now, even in this final confrontation. He hadn't batted an eyelash at her announcement, but here she was, falling apart. How stupid she was—she'd never even considered it.

She took a deep breath and spoke. "Who—"

"Someone from work."

She knew, now, where the pain of the end would come from. It wasn't from severing their union, or having to raise Thomas in a broken home, or the embarrassment of having to tell her family that she'd failed. It was the way he was looking at her now—not with fear or obligation or anger, but pure indifference. She was a stranger, and not one he particularly cared about. As if he'd only just woken up.

"Paul," she said, her voice tiny, but still intruding on the quietest Brooklyn evening in the history of Brooklyn evenings. "Do you think we should talk about—" she swallowed a lump that was forming "—who's going to get what, and things like that—"

He looked at her without saying anything. God, he was so

thin. When they were first dating, she'd forget sometimes, then remember when he was naked, leaning over the edge of the bed fumbling with a condom, and his arched back would seem to go on forever, stretching like Silly Putty.

He started to say something, but then Thomas called to them from upstairs, some indiscernible request. They looked at each other. Paul closed his eyes. She tried to guess what he was thinking.

"I'll go," he said, and left.

Thomas was beginning to think he would never see anyone disappear again. Thanksgiving seemed like a long time ago. At school they made reindeer antlers and Santa hats, but it wasn't the same. After the trip, he'd left the broken headdress in the car, and neither of his parents had bothered to tell him to bring it in.

The airplane dream had gotten worse. Instead of France, they were flying to Manhattan, which didn't make any sense because they lived in Brooklyn and the airport was in Queens, but that's how it was in the dream. And this time, he knew why they were crashing—there were huge buildings in their way, and even though he was sitting in the passenger part of the plane he could see through the front window. There were people in the building, people he knew: Miss Ackley and Ingrid and her parents and his grandparents and Uncle Joe, and his parents were there, even though they were sitting next to him on the plane, too. And everyone kept going, "This can't be happening, I can't believe it," like the people on TV, but no one did anything about it. They just let it happen.

He'd wake up and his dad would be there, only now he wouldn't be shaking him, like at first. He'd just be sitting at the foot of his bed and looking at him, really sadly. Thomas was starting to think that was the way his parents were going to look at him forever.

Finally, when he'd almost forgotten that he'd seen his mom disappear in the first place, it happened again, right before Christmas.

It was the same dream, only this time, he had a plan. It was like magic; he didn't know why he'd never thought of it before. All he had to do was get to the cockpit and tell the pilot to turn the plane around, because he knew what was going to happen. If the pilot wouldn't listen, he'd do it himself. In the dream, he knew how to fly a plane, he just didn't like to show off. But he'd do it, if it meant saving the lives of innocent people. "Everybody calm down," he said to the other people on the plane and the people in the building. "I'll fix this."

He kissed his parents on the cheek and told them to sit down and wait for him, he'd be right back. He waved to Miss Ackley and Ingrid and her parents and Grandma Betsy and Grandpa Victor and Uncle Joe through the window. They looked so scared, he almost started to cry, but he knew he had to look brave for them or he'd only make it worse. He made himself smile, and Ingrid smiled back. She turned to the others and said something he couldn't hear, but after she spoke to them they were all smiling, at least a little, and they started chanting, "Help us, Thomas." They didn't sound scared anymore, though. They sounded like they really believed he could do it.

Then he started to make his way back up the aisle towards the front of the plane, and something really weird happened. Even though he was dreaming, he remembered that the people behind him were probably turning into monsters, and that some of them were disappearing. It made him angry. Here he was, trying to save everybody, and they couldn't wait until his back was turned to start chomping their fangs and flicking their tentacles. So he whipped around, trying to catch them in the act.

"What are you doing?" everyone yelled. "Save us!"

Thomas turned around again and started back towards the front. This time he was sure he heard monsters snarling. He turned around again.

"Stop it!" everybody yelled. No one was a monster, but they almost looked like it, they were so angry. "Stop turning around and go!"

It went on and on like that. He'd get a little closer to the front, then turn around, and each time everyone on the plane and the building got angrier and yelled at him to just go, and when he'd turn back towards the front, it would be a little further away than last time.

He never got to the front, because he woke up before he got there. Then he saw something that scared him so badly he stopped breathing for a second. He almost thought he was dreaming again. Someone was standing in his doorway, looking down at him. A monster. It was dark all around the figure, so all he could see was the outline of a woman.

He stayed still and waited, not moving, not saying anything. Maybe if he stayed still long enough, the monster wouldn't notice him.

"Thomas?"

It was his mother's voice. Thomas still didn't say anything. He still couldn't see the monster's face; it could be trying to trick him. He waited for a second, and the monster took a step towards his bed. It was his mom.

He knew he should feel less scared now, but he didn't. The cold air in his room hugged him through his thin pajamas.

"Thomas, why—" She sounded sleepy, almost still asleep. "Why are you up, sweetie, what's wrong?"

"I was dreaming," he said. "And you disappeared."

She took so long to answer that he thought she might fall back asleep, just standing there at the foot of his bed. Finally she just said it back to him. "Disappeared?" Then she sat down on the end of his bed, really slowly, like she thought her body would break if she sat down too fast. "What do you mean?"

"It's OK, Mom," he said. "You don't have to keep it a secret anymore. I know about disappearing. It happens at night, when you're asleep. I've seen you."

His mom's eyes got really wide. She looked like a little girl. Thomas figured she was probably going to start crying now, too. He was used to that by now.

Then his dad appeared in the doorway of his room. "Annie?" he said, and she answered, "I'm here."

His dad looked at him and at his mom. Thomas waited for him to come to his bed and hug him and cry too, but he didn't. He wasn't even really looking at him. He was looking at his mom, and she was looking back at him, and they seemed to stay that way for a long time.

Eventually his dad went back into his room and his mom tucked him into bed and kissed his cheek. She didn't say anything except, "I'm sorry." Thomas didn't know what she was sorry for. He lay awake for the rest of the night and couldn't get back to sleep.

28

Paul listened to an NPR call-in show as he drove Thomas into Manhattan to meet Annie. The topic was, "How has America changed since the attacks on the World Trade Center?" Most of it was too mealy-mouthed for him; people seemed hesitant to say anything honest or objective, like how unpleasant flying had become because of all the new extra security measures. Only one caller echoed Paul's sentiments: "I have to tell you, it's the first week of the new year and, personally, I enjoy the fact that it's 2003 now, because it's a reminder that every day we're further and further away from 2001 and the terrible things that happened that year. To be honest, I'm really looking forward to the day when we stop harping on and on about September 11th, stop belaboring discussions like this one, when maybe we'll be able to put all this behind us and stop living in this thing's shadow, living in the past."

Paul couldn't tell if Thomas was listening or not. He decided to try to use the show as a springboard for discussion; after all, they'd never had an official Awesome Lesson about the attacks. The caller was right: almost two years had passed. Maybe it was time.

"Hey, Thomas?" He wasn't sure how to begin. "Would you—maybe we should talk a little bit about what happened that year. The airplanes and the attacks. Would you like that?"

Thomas seemed to consider the idea for a moment. Then, as if remembering something suddenly, he said, "Deirdre says I shouldn't focus on that stuff."

Deirdre was the shrink. He'd gotten her name from Ankit. They'd managed to recover from their clunky first interaction; when Paul ran into him at school functions and tried to keep his distance, to his surprise, Ankit would initiate conversations with him anyway. Paul had managed not to get quite as maudlin after that first time, but had a feeling that if he had it would have been OK. He had a theory that Ankit didn't have many friends either, although that was hard to believe. He played tennis; Paul had always thought people who played tennis seemed to lead charmed lives.

In December, Paul had looked him up in the class phone number list, called and asked if he was also stir crazy from the unnecessarily long winter break and if he'd like to get a drink. Ankit laughed and said "of course" like he completely understood, and Paul had felt so grateful he wondered for a moment if he might be in love with this man he'd only met a handful of times.

They met at a stubbornly surviving dive bar in Park Slope that they both had nostalgic associations with. They mostly talked about Ankit's New York upbringing, very different than Annie's; he'd grown up in Jackson Heights, in Queens, where his parents owned a restaurant. Something about Ankit's poise, his expensive-looking pressed shirts and khakis, the fact that he worked for a pharmaceutical company, made it hard to believe that he was such a relatable guy, even self-deprecating sometimes.

At some point in the conversation, Paul alluded to Thomas's nightmares. He left out the screaming part and anything about Annie's nighttime habits, and tried to lean heavily on the 9/11 aspect of it: the kid was still scared, and wasn't that to be expected?

"I guess," Ankit had said. From the unsure way he said it, Paul thought Ankit was going to tell him it sounded like a pretty big deal, something to be concerned about, maybe even get the whole story out of him. Instead, he said, "Joshua had nightmares and we thought the same thing for a while, until he started wetting the bed."

Later, Paul regretted being so transparently fascinated, maybe even pleased, by this piece of information. "He... your kid wet the bed? And it hadn't happened before?"

Ankit shook his head. "No. It freaked him out. It freaked *us* out." He drank his beer and was quiet for a minute. "I had just absolutely no idea what was going on. What to do."

Several possible responses, too jokey, too personal, had occurred to him. Something about the way Ankit looked when he talked about his son stopped Paul from saying more about Thomas. He did want to know what Ankit meant, exactly, by speaking in both the singular and the plural, if his wife was going through all this with him or if their relationship was strained, too. He didn't ask. *Next time*, he thought.

As delicately as he could, Paul asked him what had happened, if things were OK now.

Ankit raised his eyebrows and perked up, like he'd been looking forward to the question. "Yes, actually," he'd said. "He's seeing someone, a child, uh, psychologist, psychiatrist, I honestly can't remember which one it is, but she's great and Josh likes her very much."

Paul nodded and made congratulatory noises, then returned to his beer. "She's right in the neighborhood, too, right over on Degraw," Ankit added, and Paul nodded down at his beer. When Ankit spoke again, his voice was careful, gentle. "Paul...? Do you want me to give you her number? For Thomas?"

"Yes." He felt a rush of relief, and an accompanying urge to tell Ankit everything. "There's... there's actually a lot," he said, but then got choked up and couldn't get any more out.

Ankit raised his palm to him as he scrolled through the numbers in his cell phone. "It's OK," he said, "you don't have to tell me." He pulled over a coaster, wrote down a name and a number, and slid it over to Paul. "Really. I get it."

Paul felt warm and on the verge of weeping; there was beer in his system, and it wasn't so unusual for him to feel that way lately anyway.

"Thanks," he said, and then, afraid that he may have not conveyed enough sincerity, said again, "Thank you, Ankit."

Ankit had given his shoulder a little squeeze. "I think this could really help," he said. "And, hey, if you ever *do* want to talk about it more..." He finished the sentence by lifting his beer glass and giving Paul a meaningful look.

"Thank you," Paul said, this time feeling tears, unmistakably. "I really appreciate that." He'd been afraid, then, that they'd ventured too far into mushy territory to salvage a casual, friendly evening, but when he returned from wiping his eyes in the bathroom, they'd transitioned seamlessly into talking about baseball. It was one of the better nights Paul had had in a while.

"McEnery?" Annie had said when he showed her the coaster the next day. "That doesn't *sound* like a Jewish name."

He'd been too tired for a fight. He'd given her a look that said, *I give up, what are you talking about?*

"You sure you're OK entrusting our child's mental health to this Gentile?"

She'd been smiling. Had he said something at some point about only trusting Jewish doctors? He had no memory of that, but he didn't doubt it. He could be an idiot sometimes.

"I'm making an exception because she's Irish," he'd said. "You bring the name of a WASP doctor in here and we'll be having a different conversation."

She'd laughed at that; *I made her laugh*, he'd thought.

Thomas did like Deirdre; Paul thought he may even have a little crush on her. He hadn't met her yet, since Annie took Thomas and then picked him up on the nights when she saw her own shrink, but he felt an uncharacteristic trust in her, sight unseen, if for no other reason than the fact that Thomas had stopped screaming in his sleep.

"OK," Paul said, turning off the radio. "Your doctor's probably right. We don't have to talk about it."

"She says when I'm ready," said Thomas, "and that if I'm not ready for a while that's OK."

Paul nodded. "Sounds good," he said.

Silence sunk in between them for a minute. Thomas looked out the window, swinging his legs in front of him.

Paul still thought about leaving, although he made an effort to think of that idea as "on hold" for now. Things with Annie were, objectively, not much different, but it was hard to feel it so urgently when Thomas was doing better. He wondered if it was as easy as that: as a young man, you're ready to break up as soon as the honeymoon phase ends and you have your first fight; when you're older, married, one thing in your terrible relationship gets fixed and you'll decide that means everything's fine. He imagined that the dust would settle after a little while with Thomas's shrink, and hers, and he'd evaluate, clear-eyed and guilt-free, where things stood. He was ready.

"So, what else did you and Deirdre talk about this week?"

Thomas looked back at him and shook his head. "Sorry, Dad, but it's confidential."

Paul forced a smile. "Oh yeah? Confidential, huh? She told you what that means?"

"Yup. It means what we say in the room stays in the room."

"Right. That's a good rule. But it's confidential even from me? Even from your dad?"

Thomas sighed. "Yes, Dad. It's between me and Deirdre."

"Between you and Deirdre," Paul repeated, nodding thoughtfully. "Well, all right. But hey, old pal... if you ever want to, you can talk to me, too, OK? About, you know. You know."

Thomas looked over at him with that middle-of-the-night suspicion.

"Anything!" Paul concluded, giving his son a big smile. "Anything. You can always talk to me, your dad, about anything. That's all I meant."

Thomas held him in his wary stare for another moment, then said, "OK, Dad," and looked out the window again. He began humming to himself. Paul had never heard him do that before.

Stephen Scheckman's office was in midtown, near the Flatiron building. He was taking new patients, and had availability, of all times, on Mondays and Wednesdays. Annie had felt strange dialing the number, hearing a woman say the words "Dr. Scheckman's office," seeing his name in the directory in the lobby, strange about all of it. She didn't usually fear bad juju, but she thought surely fictionalizing a real person and then making contact with the real-life version was some form of God-defying hubris.

When she saw him in person for the first time, she found his lack of resemblance to her father annoying. Scheckman was bald and not fat, and his face was kind, but not jocular. He was, to all appearances, straitlaced, milquetoast... Paul-esque. She wondered if he was from New England, too.

But she forgot all that pretty quickly, because she liked him. In her first session, she told him about making him up, the journal exercises and his imaginary analysis of Thomas, and he actually laughed.

"I hope I can live up to all that," he said, and told her they could "keep it in mind" but that they didn't have to go into it too much if she had other things she'd rather talk about. He was good.

She knew the reality was that she wouldn't stop sleepwalking right away, but she'd wanted for it to happen anyway, as a reprieve from the past several months, an A for effort. Even though the first recovery attempt had been fictional, it still felt like an even longer time to wait now for results, more than anyone should have to. She'd try not to look at Paul's expression when he caught her by the elbow, asleep and standing at the top of the stairs, which had settled into her preferred sleepwalking destination. If Paul was disappointed or angry or guilty, it was out of her hands. She knew she was doing all she could.

Scheckman did help her—objectively, measurably—with one problem right away. During her third session, she was talking about Paul, as she did more often than not, and she mentioned that things were feeling a little better lately, since she and Thomas had started therapy. He asked her if she could remember the last time things felt OK between her and Paul—maybe not perfect, but OK.

"We... I was in a bit better spirits just after Thanksgiving."

Scheckman nodded and smiled. Whenever she responded to a question, he looked at her like she was a student who'd given the right answer. "Tell me more about that."

"I guess I... met someone." She realized how stupid it sounded before all the words came out. Or how stupid it *would* sound, when she explained.

It came out as a question. "... Paul's brother?"

Scheckman raised his eyebrows, but the rest of his expression didn't change. It was the closest he came to looking scandalized.

"I'd actually never met him before... but he was..." She couldn't say anything else. There was a lump in her throat that felt like it was blocking her airway. She put her hand over her open mouth and started to cry. He didn't interrupt her for a minute.

When she finally gulped that she was sorry and tended to herself with the tissues from the end table, he said, "What are you feeling now, talking about him? Can you talk about that a little?"

Annie thought she'd be able to answer that, but she couldn't. She shook her head and smiled at him apologetically.

"OK," Scheckman said. "That's OK. Can I ask… did anything happen between you and Paul's brother?"

"No," she said, and once she found she could speak, she sat up straight and took a deep breath. "No, not at all. He didn't even know that I had these feelings, and they're not—" she laughed, "—not based in anything. *Anything.* But I really—" She started to tear up again. "I actually really thought something was going to happen." Hearing the words out loud made her laugh. She said them again. "I actually thought something was going to happen between me and my husband's brother."

She wiped her eyes and her nose. Scheckman still said nothing, but smiled at her, silently saying that it was OK to keep talking, or to stop, whatever she needed to do. Such a kind, quiet smile. She wished she didn't have to leave after an hour. "I guess I've never said this out loud. And realized just—how—how *insane* it is. I mean, there's no other word for it! I lost my mind! I actually felt…"

"Hope," Scheckman said. His voice hit her in the chest. The entire year seemed to crash in on that moment, on the brown suede couch in the small room on the eighth floor of an office building in midtown, the white noise machine in the corner humming into oblivion.

"… is that it?" he asked.

"Yes," she said, taking a handful of tissues. "Yes, that's it exactly."

He nodded. "Tell me how that felt."

So she told him.

Joe called in March. She'd talked about him with Scheckman a fair amount but he'd tapered off as a subject of their conversations after a few weeks. She hadn't thought about him in a while. Then she heard his voice, and knew that she was a failure, and that she'd never get better.

"Hey, Annie," he said. "I was just calling to say hi, see how everyone's doing." Easy and calm but alert and engaged, thoughtful, browned by the sun, she could see him in an adobe kitchen, stretching the cord to stand outside with the phone on a little patio that looked out on a pink and gold desert.

"That is so sweet, Joe," she said. *Sweet.* She was a disgrace, a lumbering cow.

"How is everyone?"

"Oh, fine." She forced a casual note into her voice, with all her might. "You know, the holidays are stressful but we made it through another year."

What was she saying? Who was she? Her mother-in-law could come up with more interesting banter than this.

Another image of Joe came to her, of when she'd first met him, across the threshold of the terrifying house, the first friendly face she'd seen in so long. He'd been so welcoming so quickly, with no questions asked—*unconditional*, that was called. She felt a surge of guilt as she thought of Scheckman, of all that understanding, all those tissues. She shoved it down, and leaned into the feeling of that front-porch memory, an addict relapsing.

"Hey, Joe," she said. She shifted the phone from one ear to the other so that she could hold the counter with her left hand, to brace herself. "I'm glad you called. I've been thinking about what you said, about possibly taking a trip out west to see you."

She let it hang on the line. This was it.

"Oh, right!" He sounded genuinely happy, interested. "Well," he said, "the offer still stands, of course. When were you all thinking of coming out?"

Something went cold in her stomach. *You all.* She had hoped he would let her hold onto the idiotic fantasy version for at least a moment.

"Yeah," he went on. "I have to be honest, you may be more comfortable in a hotel. We have a guest room, technically, but really it's just a cot we set up in the den. But we'd still be happy to host you, I mean don't let that keep you away. We'll figure something out. I think Carly's got an air mattress somewhere."

It might have been the most he'd ever said to her at one time. She thought of the guidebook she'd bought, lying on top of her journal in the drawer of her nightstand—a drawer filled with things she didn't use anymore, but were still there, beside her every night as she slept.

He was still talking. "We're pretty in and out during the week, unfortunately, so I'm afraid we might not be the world's most attentive hosts, but we love the area, so we could give you guys plenty of ideas for places to check out nearby—"

In Scheckman's office, she had laughed when she envisioned this exact moment, how stupid it was to have concocted it as anything else. It had seemed silly. Everything, Thomas and Paul and the sleepwalking and the towers falling, it was all just a thought experiment when she talked to Scheckman, still and hanging on a wall in some other room, waiting to be analyzed. But now it was real, with the impossible, inescapable reality of a dream.

The line had gone silent for several seconds. "Hey," Joe said. "You still there?"

It was, she realized, the most intimate tone he'd ever used with her.

"Yeah," she said. "Sorry. I—got distracted. Let me get Paul for you." She heard him say something as she put the phone down and went to find her husband.

In the living room, Thomas was playing with his trucks on the carpet. He looked up at her as she came in. "Is that Uncle Joe?" he asked. "Are we going to go visit him in New Mexico?"

It was Thursday. She knew it might be a difficult weekend, until she saw Scheckman again on Monday. That would help. Sometimes there was help, and when there wasn't, life was hard, and you put your head down and did what you could.

She thought of going over to Thomas, sitting down on the carpet, getting close. But something about his little tilted head made her stay where she was. "No, sweetie," she said. "We're just going to stay here."

EPILOGUE

Thanksgiving

Thomas's alarm rang at 5:45am. It was too quiet; a silence that spread itself out over everything, beyond his room, the hall, this building, across the entire campus. Thomas stretched and wondered if he'd ever been awake this early here, if it would be completely different, the grass wet, the air the kind of cold he hadn't felt since he was back on the East Coast.

He shut off the alarm and told himself he was going to wake up, that he just needed a moment to stare at the ceiling and collect himself, but he must have fallen back asleep, because he woke to his phone vibrating next to him in the bed.

Thomas looked at the name on the screen, then answered, speaking through a yawn. "It's too early even for *you* to be up."

"It's three hours later here, my dear boy," said Ingrid. He could hear movement, kitchen sounds, in the background.

"I know. I'm saying, even with those three hours, it's too early for you to be up."

"I guess I was just full of energy because I'm so excited about this very special day."

"Shut up." He stood up, stretched some more, made some movement towards the bathroom. He was alone; his roommate had left the day before, but Gordon's side of the room looked like he had just run out for class and would be back any minute: his bed was unmade and filled with open books and dirty clothes, and there was even still some weed in the bowl on his little coffee table.

"All right, grumpy," said Ingrid. "Tell me again what time your flight gets in."

"Six."

"Six…?"

Thomas saw himself smile in the bathroom mirror. In most ways, Ingrid was the ultimate hipster, unaffected by anything, aware of and usually ahead of everything in the cultural landscape, effortlessly cool. But she also had this mothering streak, this obsession with details and a tendency to worry, that you only really got to see if you were close to her.

"Six-fourteen," he said.

"OK." There was a pause; he knew she was writing it down.

"Hey," he said, "you really do not need to pick me up at the airport. Like, you really don't."

"Ugh, Thomas, stop, we talked about this already."

"I know, but I'm saying it again."

He heard a voice in the background and knew it was Rachel, who was probably the only person he'd ever met who was cooler than Ingrid, so it made sense that they ended up together. He'd met her when they both came to Oregon the summer before and visited him. He was always sure to phrase it that way in his mind: they'd come to Oregon, and visited him while they were here; Ingrid did not take the trip *to* see him. He liked Rachel, a lot actually, and he knew it was good that Ingrid was happy, in theory.

He waited while Ingrid's voice went away, and only spoke again when he could hear her return to the phone. "What if I said I'm pretending to be considerate but really I just don't want to get into a car with you?"

"I'd say that's fine," she said, "because Rachel's driving."

Rachel was from Ohio, an honest-to-God New York success story, a girl who'd filled her Subaru with all her stuff and driven there broke and hopeful, and found a restaurant job and a girlfriend and an apartment in some offensively short amount of time. They insisted that the Subaru made their lives better for stuff like impromptu weekend trips to Montreal; Thomas still thought it was absurd to own a car in New York.

"I'd also say fuck you," Ingrid added, "because I'm a great driver."

"You're really not."

He wanted to say more, to share a memory with her about the time senior year when she was supposed to drive them into the Village and they ended up in Jersey City, or even just to poke at this more, to tease her and pretend it was flirting—maybe it *would* be flirting, in some way, just a little—but he could tell that she'd just called up to ask about the flight and that the conversation was reaching its ending. He'd see her soon, anyway, although he knew that wouldn't be the same.

He forced himself to end it. With Ingrid, every little bit of dignity helped. "OK," he said, "I gotta get ready and make this long schlep to the airport. I'll see you tonight."

"See you tonight!" she said, and he heard Rachel saying *bye Thomas* in the background.

It was hard to know what was and wasn't home. He would have asked his father, when he was little, whether his grandparents' house in New Hampshire still felt like home to him when he went back there as an adult, or if it felt like a vacation house, or something else entirely. But maybe his dad never really figured it out, like Thomas was beginning to think he never would.

He didn't know anything about his parents' heartbreaks, what they'd done to get past them, if such a thing was even possible. He had theories, but it was all speculation, based on what he'd been able to figure out when he was a kid. Most people didn't want to know that kind of stuff about their parents, and there was plenty that Thomas didn't want to get into with them, but he knew that at the very least they were an archive of emotional knowledge.

Ingrid didn't have that; her mother was dead, and her father was perpetually M.I.A., in and out of rehab and pretty much useless when he was around. Thomas had been too stupid to figure that out for himself; she'd screamed it at him when he was home for the summer after freshman year and his parents were driving him crazy. She'd called him a self-involved spoiled idiot and they hadn't spoken for the rest of the summer, just when he'd thought things were finally becoming less awkward between them. He'd really felt that she hated him, and that she was right: he was a terrible person.

"Thomas, come on, you're not a *terrible person*," she'd said when they made up, over the phone, the following fall. "You just need to pay attention."

He'd really tried, since then, to pay attention. He didn't know exactly what she'd meant, so he tried to pay attention to everything. She was that important to him.

He didn't know if the brownstone on Henry Street was still his home, but it did a decent impression of home. It didn't seem foreign, but it wasn't so familiar that just looking at it made him feel warm or safe, either.

Rachel and Ingrid used parking as an excuse when Thomas asked them, repeatedly, to come inside. "Ingrid, I know they'd really love to see you. And Rachel, they've heard a lot about you, I know they're eager to meet you finally." He felt like a noodgy aunt.

"We'll see them some time this week," Ingrid said to him as he stood outside the car with his bag, taking his hand through the window. "You should have some time alone with them first, anyway." He couldn't argue with that. She got the last word on any parent-related matters; orphan's prerogative.

At the front door, his dad hugged him before he let him walk inside. It was a tight, almost desperate hug, more appropriate for someone coming home from war than from college.

Thomas thumped his father's back a couple times. "Hi, Dad."

His father held on for a few more seconds before pulling back. "It's so good to see you. Come on, here, let me take your bag." Thomas let him take his one light duffel bag without complaint; he tried to let him feel helpful whenever he could.

His dad went to put his bag upstairs and Thomas found his mother in the kitchen. She hugged him with the same misplaced urgency as his father, but Thomas didn't mind it as much from her. He leaned into his mother's small frame; she'd been shorter than him by a few inches since high school.

She was fifty-two, with a tasteful older-woman haircut and funky earrings she'd had forever, almost tacky but not quite. She was wearing an oversized sweater and jeans; Thomas was glad to see she hadn't dressed up for his arrival. She looked comfortable.

She pulled away from him and ran her hand around the outline of his face as she stared up at him. The gesture was a little cheesy, but he didn't mind.

"Keep me company while I finish dinner," she said.

"Can I help with anything?"

"No. I want to make dinner for my prodigal son; come on, you know this."

Thomas smiled. "I do."

She disappeared under the counter as she dug around in the pots and pans cabinet. "How's Ingrid?"

"She's good."

"Yeah? She still like NYU? And, uh… oh, I forgot her name. They're still good?"

"Rachel. Yes, I mean I think, and yes, they're good."

His mother poured something into a pan and turned on the oven, then turned to him with a serious look. "It's so good that you two can spend time together again, Thomas. Really. I'm proud of you."

Thomas rubbed his forehead. "Mom, come on, we never weren't spending time together, I don't know how many times I have to explain this."

She waved her hand in front of her face, scattering his words away. "I know, I know, but you know what I mean. It was tough there for a while."

"Sure, Mom."

"Leave him alone." Thomas's father patted him on the back as he came into the kitchen and took two beers from the refrigerator. "Annie, come on, he just walked in the door." He opened the beers and gave one to Thomas.

"Thank you. It's OK, Dad."

"It is OK. He can tell me to leave me alone himself if he wants to, you don't need to rescue him."

Thomas didn't like beer, but he took a long swallow out of the brown bottle his father had handed him.

"Just, you know, give him a minute to catch his breath."

"Dad…"

"Or hey, even better, leave it alone. He's on vacation. Let him bring it up if he wants to."

"*Dad*. It's *OK*."

"Listen to him, Paul. You've made your point. You're not impressing anyone with this."

Thomas took a deep breath through his nose. "Hey. Everybody. Everything's fine. OK? Everything is OK."

To Thomas's relief, they both stood down. It didn't always dissipate that quickly.

"Garlic bread," his dad said suddenly, after they shared a silence for a while. "I've gotta make the garlic bread, I almost forgot."

"*You're* making something?" Thomas asked.

"I cook all the time."

"Since when?"

Annie smiled. "We've been making meals together for a while now, actually. You know, he's not bad."

"She's right, I'm not!" His father peeled a garlic clove. "I used to cook more, at other points in my life."

Thomas made an exaggeratedly impressed face and nodded slowly. "Well, all right. Dad cooking."

"That's right," said his father. "And don't be a little jerk about it."

Thomas put up his palms in a sign of surrender. "OK. Well. You guys make your meal, don't let me interfere. I really need a shower."

As Thomas walked up the stairs, his father said something he couldn't hear, and his mother laughed.

At dinner, his father started in right away. "So, Thomas. How are you doing?"

Thomas frowned at his father over his pasta. It wasn't just a stiff, generic question. It was extremely specific. "I am fine," Thomas said, slowly and loudly. "I have *been* fine. Dad, I thought I was on vacation, remember?"

His mother put her fork down and sighed, but didn't say anything.

"You know, sometimes we can't really get a sense of things on the phone," his dad said. "So now that you're here, you know, we should talk about it."

Thomas rubbed his eyes. He hated this, but he wasn't surprised. He knew what they wanted to hear: that not only was he all better since the episode this summer, but that he was now equipped to fully explain it. They wanted a full report on the origins of his sudden, insatiable cleanliness; his insistence, when his room-mate woke up to discover Thomas cleaning the apartment at four in the morning, that there were insects, an infestation of some kind, even though neither of them had actually seen any insects, or any evidence that pointed to them. He'd refused to stop clean-ing, and eventually Gordon had relented and gone back to bed. Then Thomas found a spider in the bathroom, and Gordon had to check him into the emergency psych ward in the middle of the night. They wanted to know why.

He knew that his being better was secondary to being able to account for his behavior. They liked answers. He had told them, so many times, that nothing like this had happened since then, that he'd talked to a campus shrink about it, that she'd given him some practical advice and he'd taken it, that he was handling it. It wasn't enough for them. It would never be enough.

His first instinct was to tell his parents that he'd calmed down con-siderably since he'd started smoking pot pretty often, but he decided it wasn't worth whatever conversation that would provoke. "I really am fine," he said. "That's all I can say about it, OK?"

There was more to say. He could have told them that he'd started volunteering at a school in Portland for little kids with developmental disabilities; that it made him feel happier than he had in a long time, too long; that it weirdly made him feel *safer* than he'd felt in a long time, the opposite of the empty terror he'd felt during that 4am bug scare. He could have told them that he was thinking about becoming a teacher, that he'd pretty much decided he was going to do it. But he didn't want to give them the satisfaction of such packaged good news, something they could brag to their friends about, patting themselves on the back for having raised an upstanding son after all. He'd tell them eventually.

"I can't force you to talk about this with us, Thomas," his father said. "But... you know, it's not like this is the first time something like this has happened. I think it makes sense that we're concerned."

His father was looking at him with a sad condescension he

despised, like he was an invalid. He let his gaze travel up to his dad's half-gray hair. "Salt and pepper," that's what it was called. His dad's new look weirded him out; he looked like Mitt Romney. Tonight, he was wearing a crisp red polo shirt with a little crocodile over the pocket. He'd gotten new glasses with plastic frames, nearly identical to what a lot of guys at school wore. Guys Thomas's age. Thomas wondered if this was also some marriage therapy recommendation, that he should spruce himself up for his wife. It seemed so unlike his parents to go for that kind of thing. Maybe it was just a byproduct of having so much more money to throw around, between getting tenure and selling the house in New Hampshire after Grandma Betsy died the year before. That explanation was a little gross, but Thomas preferred it to thinking of his father's new wardrobe as some kind of marital aid.

"Freshman year," Thomas said. "That was two years ago. And, yeah, then again last summer. That's it. It's not like it's happening every week."

He looked over at his mother. She was silent, staring down at her food. She looked like she was about to cry.

He was about to say more when his mother spoke. "Paul," she said, "please. Leave it."

Thomas braced himself for a repeat of the same argument from before. His father took a deep breath—dramatically deep. *Here we go*, Thomas thought.

"You're right," his dad said. He looked at his mom for a long moment before he turned back to Thomas. "We don't have to talk about anything you don't want to."

His mother was smiling at his father; Thomas felt like he was intruding on something. After a moment, they both resumed eating. "Thanks, Dad," he said. His father offered only a muted nod in response.

After dinner, they watched TV together. Thomas sat in his dad's old chair and his parents sat together on the couch.

He met up with Rachel and Ingrid near NYU and they went to a coffee shop in the West Village that had opened some time after

Thomas left. It was tiny and clean and pretty much interchangeable with most of the coffee shops in Portland. He'd never really appreciated his mother's laments about how much New York had changed until he came back from being away, and huge chunks of what he remembered would be gone.

At some point Rachel checked her phone and announced that she had to get to work. She put her arm around Ingrid, squeezed her and kissed her cheek. They were about the same size, but Ingrid looked waifish in Rachel's muscular arms, tattoos poking out from under the sleeves of her faded t-shirt. Rachel would have fit in perfectly in Portland, too, in her beanie and gauge earrings. She was like a Universal Barista. He couldn't hold that against her, though; he always got along well with those baristas. When Rachel hugged Thomas, she rubbed his back a little where a man might have thumped, and he thought the pressure of her arms conveyed a sincerity that he appreciated.

"You kids have fun," she said, disappearing up Seventh Avenue.

"I'm hungry," said Ingrid. "Do you wanna go to our diner?"

He wasn't sure how to feel about her referring to the place on Smith Street that they'd been going to after school since they were thirteen as *our diner*. He'd done a lot of work to stop considering things as belonging to the two of them. But he guessed this was part of the stage they were in now, her more firmly than him, where the past was the past and they were doing just fine.

On the F to Bergen Street, he told her he was jealous that she was still in New York, that he missed it constantly.

"That's not good," she said. "Wasn't that the whole point of the West-Coast-for-college idea? Get as far away as possible?"

"Of course. And I stand by that decision. But, you know, that plan's really ideal for someone who grew up in some shitty small town."

Ingrid nodded at him and he could tell she was absorbing what he was saying, trying to fully get a handle on it before she offered a response; really listening, the way she'd been listening since they were little kids. "New York never did anything to you," she said after a moment. Thomas knew there was an implied question in there; *did I get that right?*

"Yes. Exactly."

At the diner, they ordered grilled cheese sandwiches and Thomas got a nostalgic egg cream. When the food came, he automatically handed Ingrid his cup of soggy coleslaw.

They exchanged stories about the various disappointing stupid people they'd encountered at their respective colleges, and the few good people who'd floated to the surface too. Ingrid admitted she sometimes used Rachel as an excuse not to meet new people or explore potential friendships.

"That's not, like, wildly surprising," Thomas said. "I mean, look who you're talking to."

She smiled. "We were always kind of 'us against the world,' huh."

He didn't say anything. He knew she was talking about their fifteen years of friendship, and not the year—less than a year—when they were dating, or hooking up or experimenting or however it was they were supposed to think about it. This was when it was hardest, though; when she said things that could, in some light, mean more.

When they'd paid the check and he was about to stand up, Ingrid said his name with a seriousness that made him sit back down. He tried to tamp down the stupid swell of hope he felt.

"I just wanted to say I'm really glad that we're hanging out again," she said. "That it's not awkward and that we're friends like we used to be. You're so important to me, you know? And I really missed you."

He wanted to laugh. He didn't tell her it was almost verbatim what his annoying, nosy mother had said. He also didn't get into a really honest response either: it wasn't not awkward, not for him, and it wasn't like it used to be. It wasn't all better, despite what everyone but him seemed to think. It still hurt.

But there they were, at their diner, and that was something.

"Me too, Ingrid," he said.

Then she took the G train and he walked down Smith Street back to his parents' house. He stood in the front hallway. It was quiet. His parents were somewhere inside; he couldn't hear them, but he knew they were there.

Acknowledgements

Of course, first and foremost, I can't thank my donors enough for making this happen, believing in me and helping me out. Some of you are people I haven't seen in years; some of you are strangers! I feel tremendously grateful to all of you whenever I think about this project, which I honestly didn't think would ever reach this stage. Thank you.

Additional thanks are owed to Nurbek Ismailov, a donor whose name didn't make it to the list; to Xander, Annabel, Elizabeth, Elodie, Molly and Leonora at Unbound, Mark Ecob at Mecob Design, and to the community of Unbound authors I was able to connect with through social media, all of whom generously fielded my questions and helped me through this confusing, exciting process.

Thanks to Roy Marin, for lending his talents to my promotional video and for being a pretty all right guy; I love ya, ya film school knucklehead. To the brilliant and kind Janet Skeslien Charles, for interviewing me and also for encouraging me and my writing since I was nineteen (!). And to my dear friend Ben Wellington, for help above and beyond, and for being impressed enough with my squirrel impression many years ago to change my life a little bit.

Danelle Knapp, Silke Anderson, Veronica Hapgood, and Amy Ferlazzo, thank you for being there and believing in me, in book-related matters and otherwise. Thanks to Pete Williams, for being so welcoming and generous, and for countless delicious meals when I might otherwise have had peanut butter for dinner; and to Juliette and Lucy, who have big hearts and are a lot of fun, even when they're making me feel old.

One friend I mentioned in these acknowledgements has passed away since I originally wrote them. Ciaran McCabe was kind, charismatic, and deviously funny. Many of us met Ciaran when we were nine or ten years old, and we were lucky to meet him then, because he was so gifted at making us feel special, seen and heard, and loved. We'll all miss him a lot.

To my parents, Rita Sherry and Peter Weissman: thank you both for all the parts of myself I like best. I love you, and I'm glad (most of the time) to be a part of our strange little family.

And to my chosen family, Melani Baker, Lisa Baker, and Joe Leonard, the kindest, smartest people I've ever known, for everything.

Patrons

Erin Baer
Sally Blanchard-O'Brien
Sauce Chalice
Mallory Clarke
Julie Cochran
Brian Danielak
Elizabeth Devlin
Jared Gottlieb
Colleen Grotzky
Jeniece Ilkowitz
Toasha Jiordano
Laura Kerrigan
Amy Keyes
Dan Kitrosser
Adam Leier
Jessica Mcconnell
Emily Mitchell-Eaton
Cordelia Ochis
Tricia Pierce
DC Pierson
Saswati Samantaray
Scott Schwartz
Helen Staab
Sarah Strasen
Chill Wave
Hannah Whelan